Israel Smith Clare, John H. Landis

The Life of James Gillespie Blaine

Israel Smith Clare, John H. Landis

The Life of James Gillespie Blaine

ISBN/EAN: 9783337103941

Printed in Europe, USA, Canada, Australia, Japan

Cover: Foto ©Raphael Reischuk / pixelio.de

More available books at **www.hansebooks.com**

THE LIFE

OF

JAMES GILLESPIE BLAINE.

BY

JOHN H LANDIS

AND

ISRAEL SMITH CLARE.

LANCASTER, PA.
THE NEW ERA PRINTING HOUSE.
1884.

Dedicated to

THE YOUNG MEN OF THE COUNTRY,

WHO ARE WILLING TO DEVOTE THEIR BEST ENERGIES

IN ADVANCING THE CAUSE FOR WHICH

JAMES A. GARFIELD DIED.

TABLE OF CONTENTS:

JAMES GILLESPIE BLAINE.

JAMES GILLESPIE BLAINE was born January 31, 1830, at the Indian Hill Farm, Washington county, Pennsylvania, opposite the town of Brownsville. The old stone house in which he was born is yet standing, and is now included within the limits of West Brownsville—though at the time of his birth it was only the mansion house of the Gillespie farm. The house was erected by Mrs. Blaine's great-grandfather, the elder Neal Gillespie, in 1778, on what was then the western frontier of civilization. The late James L. Bowman, of Brownsville, who was conversant with the history of that locality, said it was the first stone house ever erected on the western side of the Monongahela river.

Mr. Blaine entered public life by a strong association in his immediate family, if not by a law of heredity. His great-grandfather, Colonel Ephraim Blaine, of Carlisle, Cumberland county, Pennsylvania, held the position of Commissary-general of the American army during the War of the Revolution, from the year 1778 to the end of the struggle in 1783.

Mr. Blaine's grandfather, for whom he is named, intended at first to choose a professional and political career, but a somewhat protracted stay in Europe, after he had finished his studies, directed him from the line of his first and better ambition, as has been the case

2

with many young Americans. He returned to his home
in 1793, bringing with him, as special bearer of des-
patches, a famous treaty with a foreign power, since
become memorable; and subsequently, chiefly followed
the life of a private gentleman. Mr. Blaine's father
was born and reared in Carlisle, and after an extensive
tour in Europe, South America, and the West Indies,
returned to spend most of his life in Washington
county, Pennsylvania, where he died before his son had
reached manhood. He came to Western Pennsylvania about the year 1818, being the owner of larger
landed possessions than any other man of his age in
that section of the State. His estate, if it had been
preserved intact, would to-day have been worth many
millions of dollars.

In 1825, Mr. Ephraim L. Blaine (the father of the
subject of our sketch) deeded to the Economites the
splendid tract now occupied by the city of Pittsburg,
with all its improvements and all its wealth. The
price was $25,000 for a property, which at the present
day, if even not improved, would be valued at millions. There were likewise timber tracts on the Alle-
gheny river and coal lands on the Monongahela, then
of no special value, which represent large fortunes in
the hands of their present owners. Very near the
large tracts owned by his father and grandfather, Mr.
Blaine now owns one of the most highly valuable coal
tracts in the Monongahela valley. In extent it is but
a part of what he might have hoped to inherit, but in
value it is much greater than the entire landed property of his father fifty years ago.

Mr. Blaine's father took special pains to give his
son a thorough intellectual training. He was under
the best tutorage in his earliest years, and at the age

of eleven was sent to school at Lancaster, Ohio, where he lived in the family of his relative, the Hon. Thomas Ewing, then Secretary of the Treasury. General Thomas Ewing, recently in Congress, Mr. Blaine's cousin, of the same age, was his classmate, under the tuition of William Lyons, an Englishman, a brother of the elder Lord Lyons and uncle of the Lord Lyons lately British Minister at Washington.

Mr. Blaine's father, having been unfortunate in business when elected Prothonotary of the County Court in 1842 (five years before Mr. Blaine graduated), was poor, and only a Justice of the Peace. Of his five sons, James was the third, and his daughter was married to Robert J. Walker, also a graduate of Washington College. His father's new office caused him to remove to the county-seat, and enabled him to send James to college, which under the circumstances he would have been otherwise unable to do. James entered the freshmen class of Washington college, in November, 1843, and graduated in September, 1847, at the age of 17 years and 8 months. In a class of thirty-three, Mr. Blaine shared the first honor with John C. Hervey, now Superintendent of Public Instruction at Wheeling.

At the quarter-centennial of the class, in 1872, twenty-nine of the thirty-three members were living, and all were men of position and character in their respective communities. John H. Hampton, Esq., of Pittsburg, A. M. Gow, of Washington, Pa., and John V. Lemoyne, of Chicago, were members of the class.

At college, Mr. Blaine was a most excellent student. Mr. Blaine was assigned the Latin salutatory, in which he acquitted himself very well as a classical student; and he showed, in a most marked degree, the

qualities, with examples of which he has since dazzled
the country, of quick apprehension of all advantages
and difficulties in his road and perfect command of
all his resources for instantaneous use. His ability to
give utterance to anything he had to say in the most
forcible way was also noticeable in his wrangles or
political discussions with his fellow-students. His absolute self-command under difficulties here also exhibited themselves distinctly in his character. He was
the most skillful mathematician in his class, and frequently would demonstrate the problem in a way not
found in the books. It was a common occurrence for
the old teacher of mathematics to say : " Mr. Blaine,
you are not demonstrating that in the proper way."
Mr. Blaine would readily reply : " I know I am not,
sir; but give me a chance to work it out, and you'll
see it come out all right." And it did " come out all
right."

Mr. Blaine's fondness for politics was shown at this
early age in so marked a manner that his associates
recollect it distinctly. In 1847 he graduated. This
was three years after the Polk and Clay Presidential
campaign. Young Blaine was an ardent Clay man,
admiring his hero so much that it has been suspected
that he got some of his peculiar powers from a study
of the life, character, and speeches of " Young Harry
of the West." It is now universally asserted by
those who knew Henry Clay in the Speaker's chair at
Washington, that Mr. Blaine follows his footsteps so
closely in ability as a presiding officer that he " gibes
his heel." Blaine, consequently, was always the court
of last resort in a political discussion as to facts or
opinions, because he was far above every one else in
college as to knowledge of politics.

When young Blaine left college he was without means, as his father's earnings as Prothonotary were almost insufficient to maintain his large family, and the youthful graduate went to Kentucky to teach school in the country. He afterwards taught there in an academy, until he met his present wife, who was likewise a teacher in a school in Kentucky. She was a Maine woman, and after his marriage Mr. Blaine followed his bride to her own home in the Pine Tree State and settled there—thus going contrary to Horace Greeley's advice, by going East instead of going West. Mr. Blaine had meantime written for the newspapers and magazines, and studied law, though he never entered upon the practice of that profession.

BLAINE IN MAINE.

When he went to Maine, in 1853, he became editor of the Kennebec *Journal*, and afterward of the Portland *Advertiser*. He was elected to the Maine Legislature in 1858, and served in that capacity four years, the last two as Speaker of the House of Representatives.

The following paragraph is from a letter by the late Governor Kent, of Maine :

"Almost from the day of his assuming editorial charge of the Kennebec *Journal*, at the early age of 23, Mr. Blaine sprang into a position of great influence in the politics and policy of Maine. At 25 he was a leading power in the councils of the Republican party, so recognized by Fessenden, Hamlin, and the two Morrills, and others then and still prominent in the State. Before he was 29 he was chosen Chairman of the Executive Committee of the Republican organization in Maine—a position he has held ever since, and from which he has practically shaped and directed every political campaign in the State—always leading his party to brilliant victory. Had Mr. Blaine been New-England born, he would probably not have received such rapid advancement at so early an age, even with the same ability he possessed. But there was a sort of Western *dash* about him that took with us Down-Easters—an expression of frankness, candor, and confidence that gave him, from the start, a very strong and permanent hold on our people, and, as the foundation of all, pure character and a masterly ability equal to all demands made upon him."

CAREER IN CONGRESS.

In 1862 Mr. Blaine was elected a Representative in Congress, and from that day to the present he has been known to the whole country. On the floor of the House, in the Speaker's chair, again on the floor of the House, thence into the Senate, and during the political campaigns of all these years on the stump in almost every Northern State, Mr. Blaine has been most decidedly with the people and of the people. His views on all public questions have been pronounced, sometimes to aggressiveness, and his bitterest foe has never charged him with evading or avoiding any responsibility or the expression of his conviction on any issue of the day. Though young when he entered Congress Mr. Blaine made his mark at once. At the period of darkest depression in the war, when anxiety brooded everywhere and boded everything, Mr. Blaine delivered a speech on "The Ability of the American People to Suppress the Rebellion," which was warmly commended and circulated as a campaign document during the Presidential campaign of 1864.

The delivery of this speech and some discussions soon after caused Thaddeus Stevens to say that " Blaine of Maine has shown as great aptitude and ability for the higher walks of public life as any man that had come to Congress during his period of service."

During the first session of Mr. Blaine's service in Congress, as member of the Post-Office Committee, he took an active part in co-operation with the chairman, the Hon. John B. Alley, and the late James Brooks of New York, in encouraging and securing the system of postal cars now in universal use. Distribution on the cars had not been attempted on any great scale, and the first appropriations for the enlarged service were not granted without opposition.

The following is a speech of Mr. Blaine on Maine, in reply to reflections cast on her by S. S. Cox of Ohio, in the House, June 2, 1864 :

If there be a State in this Union that can say with truth that her Federal connection confers no special benefit of a material character, that State is Maine. And yet, sir, no State is more attached to the Federal Union than Maine. Her affection and her pride are centered in the Union, and God knows she has contributed of her best blood and treasure without stint in supporting the war for the Union ; and she will do so to the end. But she resents, and I, speaking for her, resent the insinuation that she derives any undue advantage from Federal legislation, or that she gets a single dollar that she does not pay back. * * * I have spoken in vindication of a State that is as independent and as proud as any within the limits of the Union. I have spoken for a people as high-toned and as honorable as can be

found in the wide world—many of them my constituents, who are as manly and as brave as ever
faced the ocean's storms. So long, sir, as I have a
seat on this floor, the State of Maine shall not be
slandered by the gentleman from Ohio, or by gentlemen from any other State.

The following are the remarks of Mr. Blaine on
Fishing Bounties, in the House, June 2, 1864 :

A great deal has been said recently in the other
end of the Capitol in regard to the fishing bounties,
a portion of which is paid to Maine. I have a word
to say on that matter, and I may as well say it here.
According to the records of the Navy Department,
the State of Maine has sent into the naval service
since the beginning of this war six thousand skilled
seamen, to say nothing of the trained and invaluable
officers she has contributed to the same sphere of
patriotic duty. For these men the State has received
no credit whatever on her quotas for the Army. If
you will calculate the amount of bounty that would
have been paid to that number of men had they enlisted in the Army, instead of entering the Navy, as
they did without bounty, you will find it will foot up
a larger sum than Maine has received in fishing
bounties for the past twenty years. Thus, sir, the
original proposition on which fishing bounties were
granted—that they would build up a hardy and skillful class of mariners for the public defense in time
of public danger—has been made good a hundred
and a thousand-fold by the experience and the developments of this war.

The following are remarks of Mr. Blaine on Maine's
loyalty, June 21, 1864 :

The sentiment of Maine is loyal to the core, and she has shown her loyalty by complying with patriotic readiness to all demands thus far made upon her for soldiers to recruit the Army, or for sailors to man the Navy.

The next are remarks of Mr. Blaine on the Conscription Bill, June 21, 1864 :

A conscription is a hard thing at best, Mr. Speaker, but the people of this country are patriotically willing to submit to one in this great crisis for the great cause at stake. There is no necessity, however, for making it absolutely merciless and sweeping. I say, in my judgment, there is no necessity for making it so, even if there were no antecedent question as to the expediency and practicability of the measure. I believe the law as it stands, allowing commutation and substitution, is sufficiently effective, if judiciously enforced. It will raise a large number of men by its direct operation, and it will secure a very large amount of money with which to pay bounties to volunteers.

*   *   *   *   *   *   *   *   *

I cannot refrain from asking gentlemen around me, whether in their judgment the pending measure, if submitted to the popular vote, would receive the support of even a respectable minority in any district in the loyal States? Just let it be understood that whoever the lot falls on *must go*, regardless of all business considerations, all private interests, all personal engagements, all family obligations ; that the draft is to be sharp, decisive, final and inexorable, without commutation and without substitution, and my word for it you will create consternation in all the loyal States. Such a conscription was never resorted to but once, even in the French Empire under the absolutism of the first Napoleon; and for the Congress of the United States to attempt its enforcement upon their constituents is to ignore the first principles of republican and representative government.

When the Enrollment Bill was under consideration in the House, February 21, 1865, Mr. Blaine moved to amend the second section thereof by adding the following: *Provided*, That in any call for troops, no county, town, township, ward, precinct or election district, shall have credit except for men actually furnished on said call, or preceding call, by said county, town, township, ward, precinct, or election district, and mustered into the military or naval service on the quota thereof.

In favor of this amendment, among other things, Mr. Blaine said: Throughout the whole country we hear of substitute brokers selling these credits, obtained in some mysterious way, as one would sell town scrip in the market; and from this source has risen a large number of those constructive "paper credits" against which my amendment is leveled, and which, for the future, it will prevent. It may not be in our power to remedy the wrong practices of the past, but from this time forward we can guard against the repetition of these practices. We can deal with equal and exact justice to all men and to all sections; and, above all, we can deal justly by the Government in its struggle for existence. In its hour of peril it calls for men—living, active, resolute men, and it is worse than madness to answer this call with anything else than men.

Let me say in conclusion, Mr. Speaker, that noth-

ing so discourages and disheartens the brave men
at the front as the belief that proper measures are not
adopted at home for re-enforcing and sustaining them.
Even a lukewarmness or a backwardness in that respect is enough; but when you add to that the sus-
picion that unfair devices have been resorted to by
those charged with filling quotas, you naturally influence the prejudices and passions of our veterans in
the field in a manner calculated to lessen their personal zeal and generally to weaken the discipline of
the army. After four years of such patriotic and heroic effort for national unity as the world has never
witnessed before, we cannot now afford to have the
great cause injured or its fair fame darkened by a
single unworthy incident connected with it. The improper practices of individuals cannot disgrace or de-
grade the nation; but after these practices are brought
to the attention of Congress, we shall assuredly be
disgraced and degraded if we fail to apply the requisite remedy when that remedy is in our power. Let
us, then, in this hour of triumph to the national arms
do our duty here, our duty to the troops in the field,
our duty to our constituents at home, and our duty,
above all, to our country, whose existence has been in
such peril in the past, but whose future of greatness
and glory seems now so assured and so radiant.

Following the war, and throughout the Reconstruction period, Mr. Blaine was active, energetic and
intelligent. He was especially prominent in shaping
some of the most important features of the Fourteenth
Constitutional Amendment, particularly that relating
to the basis of representation. The discussions on
this great series of questions, in which Mr. Blaine
figured prominently, are among the most interesting

and valuable in the history of the Congress of the
United States of America.

Blaine declared for Protection, in the House, February 1, 1866, as will be seen in the following remarks :

In theory and in practice, I am for protecting
American industry in all its forms, and to this end
we must encourage American manufactures, and we
must equally encourage American commerce.

Following is Mr. Blaine's speech on "What the
Government Owes Its Subjects," in the House, December 10, 1866 :

Among the most solemn duties of a sovereign
government is the protection of those citizens who,
under great temptations and amid great perils, maintain their faith and their loyalty. The obligation on
the Federal Government to protect the loyalists of
the South is supreme, and they must take all needful
means to assure that protection. Among the most
needful is the gift of free suffrage, and that must be
guaranteed. There is no protection you can extend
to a man so effective and conclusive as the power to
protect himself. And in assuring protection to the
loyal citizen you assure permanency to the Government; so that the bestowal of suffrage is not merely
the discharge of a personal obligation toward those
who are enfranchised, but it is the most far-sighted
provision against social disorder, the surest guaranty
for peace, prosperity and public justice.

In 1867, while Mr. Blaine was absent in Europe,
the theory of paying the public debt in greenbacks
was started in Ohio by Mr. Pendleton and in Massachusetts by General Butler. Just after his return, in
the fall of 1867, at a special adjourned session of

Congress, in November, Mr. Blaine assaulted the proposition in a speech of great research, force and logic. Thus he was the first man in either branch of Congress who spoke against the financial heresy that has since occupied public attention. Since that time, both in Congress and before the people, Mr. Blaine has been untiring in educating public opinion to the right standard of financial and national honor. Others may have been more prominent than he in Congress, but Mr. Blaine, more than any other man, has reached the mind and aroused the popular judgment by addresses from the stump through the East and the West.

The following are remarks of Mr. Blaine on Grant, in the House, Dec. 10, 1868:

General Grant's Administration will have high vantage ground from the day of its inauguration. Its responsibilities will indeed be great, its power will be large, its opportunities will be splendid; and to meet them all we have a tried and true man, who adds to his other great elements of strength that of perfect trust and confidence on the part of the people. And to re-assure ourselves of his executive character, if re-assurance were necessary, let us remember that great military leaders have uniformly proved the wisest, firmest and best of civil rulers. Cromwell, William III., Charles XII., Frederick of Prussia, are not more conspicuous instances in monarchical governments than Washington, Jackson and Taylor have proved in our own. Whatever, therefore, may lie before us in the untrodden and often beclouded path of the future—whether it be financial embarrassment, or domestic trouble of another and

more serious type, or misunderstandings with foreign
nations, or the extension of our flag and our
sovereignty over insular or continental possessions,
North or South, that fate or fortune may peacefully
offer to our ambition—let us believe with all confidence that General Grant's administration will meet
every exigency, with the courage, the ability and
the conscience which American nationality and
Christian civilization demand.

SPEAKER OF THE HOUSE.

On the 4th of March, 1869, James G. Blaine was
elected Speaker of the House of Representatives, being
then in his 39th year. The vote stood: For James
G. Blaine, of Maine, 135 votes; for Michael C. Kerr,
of Indiana, 57 votes.

Upon taking the chair, Mr. Blaine addressed the
House, as follows:

Gentlemen of the House of Representatives: I
thank you profoundly for the great honor which you
have just conferred upon me. The gratification which
this signal mark of your confidence brings to me finds
its only drawback in the diffidence with which I assume the weighty duties devolved upon me. Succeed-
ing to a chair made illustrious by the services of such
eminent statesmen and skilled parliamentarians as
CLAY, and STEVENSON, and POLK, and WINTHROP, and
BANKS, and GROW, and COLFAX, I may well distrust
my ability to meet the just expectations of those who
have shown me such marked partiality. But relying,
gentlemen, on my honest purpose to perform all my
duties faithfully and fearlessly, and trusting in a large
measure to the indulgence which I am sure you will

always extend to me, I shall hope to retain, as I have secured your confidence, your kindly regard and your generous support.

The Forty-first Congress assembles at an auspicious period in the history of our government. The splendid and impressive ceremonial which we have just witnessed in another part of the Capitol appropriately symbolizes the triumphs of the past and the hopes of the future. A great chieftain, whose sword at the head of gallant and victorious armies saved the republic from dismemberment and ruin, has been fitly called to the highest civic honor which a grateful people can bestow. Sustained by a Congress that so ably represents the loyalty, the patriotism, and the personal worth of the nation, the President this day inaugurated will assure to the country an administration of purity, fidelity and prosperity; an era of liberty regulated by law, and of law thoroughly inspired with liberty.

Congratulating you, gentlemen, upon the happy auguries of the day, and invoking the gracious blessing of Almighty God on the arduous and responsible labors before you, I am now ready to take the oath of office and enter upon the discharge of the duties to which you have called me. [Applause.]

The oath of office was then administered to the Speaker-elect by Hon. Elihu B. Washburne, of Illinois, the senior member of the body.

On the 3d of March, 1871, the 41st Congress expired. On that day Mr. S. S. Cox, of New York, offered the following resolution:

Resolved, In view of the difficulties involved in the performance of the duties of the presiding officer of this House, and of the able, courteous, dignified, and impartial discharge of those duties by Hon. J. G. Blaine during the present Congress, it is eminently becoming that our thanks be and they are hereby tendered to the Speaker thereof.

The resolution was agreed to.

Speaker Blaine, in adjourning the House at noon of that day, said :

Gentlemen of the House of Representatives: Our labors are at an end ; but I delay the final adjournment long enough to return my most profound and respectful thanks for the commendation which you have been pleased to bestow upon my official course and conduct.

In a deliberative body of this character a presiding officer is fortunate if he retains the confidence and steady support of his political associates. Beyond that you give me the assurance that I have earned the respect and good-will of those from whom I am separated by party lines. Your expressions are most grateful to me, and are most gratefully acknowledged.

The Congress whose existence closes with this hour enjoys a memorable distinction. It is the first in which all the States have been represented on this floor since the baleful winter that preceded our late bloody war. Ten years have passed since then—years of trial and of triumph ; years of wild destruction and years of careful rebuilding ; and after all, and as the result of all, the National Government is here to-day, united, strong, proud, defiant and just, with a territorial area vastly expanded, and with three additional States represented on the folds of its flag. For these prosperous fruits of our great struggle let us humbly give thanks to the God of battles and to the Prince of Peace.

And now, gentlemen, with one more expression of the obligation I feel for the considerate kindness with which you have always sustained me, I perform the only remaining duty of my office, in declaring, as I now do, that the House of Representatives of the Forty-first Congress is adjourned without day. [Great applause.]

When the Forty-second Congress convened on the 4th day of March, 1871, Hon. James G. Blaine was re-elected Speaker of the House of Representatives, the vote standing as follows :

James G. Blaine, of Maine, received 126 votes.
Geo. W. Morgan, of Ohio, received   92   "

After Mr. Blaine had been conducted to the chair he addressed the House, as follows :

Gentlemen: The Speakership of the American House of Representatives has always been esteemed as an enviable honor.   A re-election to the position carries with it peculiar gratification, in that it implies an approval of past official bearing.   For this great mark of your confidence I can but return to you my sincerest thanks, with the assurance of my utmost devotion to the duties which you call upon me to discharge.

Chosen by the party representing the political majority in this House, the Speaker owes a faithful allegiance to the principles and the policy of that party.   But he will fall far below the honorable requirements of his station if he fails to give to the minority their full rights under the rules which he is called upon to administer.   The successful working

3

of our grand system of government depends largely
upon the vigilance of party organizations, and the
most wholesome legislation which this House pro-
duces and perfects is that which results from opposing forces mutually eager and watchful and well-nigh
balanced in numbers.

The Forty-second Congress assembles at a period
of general content, happiness and prosperity throughout the land.   Under the wise administration of the
National Government, peace reigns in all our borders,
and the only serious misunderstanding with any
foreign power is, we may hope, at this moment in
process of honorable, cordial and lasting adjustment.
We are fortunate in meeting at such a time, in representing such constituencies, in legislating for such a
country.

Trusting, gentlemen, that our official intercourse
may be free from all personal asperity, believing that
all our labors will eventuate for the public good, and
craving the blessing of Him without whose aid we
labor in vain, I am now ready to proceed with the
further organization of the House; and, as the first
step thereto, I will myself take the oath prescribed
by the Constitution and laws.   [Loud applause.]

The oath of office was then administered by Hon.
H. L. Dawes, of Massachusetts, who served longest
continuously as a member of the House.

On the 16th of March, 1871, the House considered
a resolution providing for an investigation into alleged
outrages perpetrated upon loyal citizens of the South;
when Mr. Butler, of Mass., indulged in criticisms
upon the Speaker for being the author of the resolution, and for being mainly responsible for its adoption
by a caucus of Republican members of the House;

whereupon Mr. Blaine felt called upon to leave the chair and take the floor in his defense, when the following colloquy ensued between Mr. Blaine and Mr. Butler:

MR. BLAINE, the Speaker. [Mr. Wheeler, of New York, in the chair.] I desire to ask the gentleman from Massachusetts (Mr. Butler) whether he denies to me the right to have drawn that resolution?

MR. BUTLER. I have made no assertion on that subject one way or the other.

MR. BLAINE. Did not the gentleman distinctly know that I drew it?

MR. BUTLER. No, sir.

MR. BLAINE. Did I not take it to the gentleman and read it to him?

MR. BUTLER. Yes, sir.

MR. BLAINE. Did I not show him the manuscript?

MR. BUTLER. Yes, sir.

MR. BLAINE. In my own handwriting?

MR. BUTLER. No, sir.

MR. BLAINE. And at his suggestion I added these words: "and the expenses of said committee shall be paid from the contingent fund of the House of Representatives," [Applause;] and the fact that ways and means were wanted to pay the expenses was the only objection he made to it.

MR. BUTLER. What was the answer the gentleman made? I suppose I may ask that, now that the Speaker has come upon the floor.

MR. BLAINE. The answer was that I immediately wrote the amendment providing for the payment of the expenses of the committee.

MR. BUTLER. What was my answer? Was it not

that under no circumstances would I have anything to do with it, being bound by the action of the caucus?

Mr. Blaine. No, sir; the answer was that under no circumstances would you serve as chairman.

Mr. Butler. Or have anything to do with the resolution.

Mr. Blaine. There are two hundred and twenty-four members of the House of Representatives. A committee of thirteen can be found without the gentleman from Massachusetts being on it. His service is not essential to the constitution of the committee.

Mr. Butler. Why did you not find such a committee, then?

Mr. Blaine. Because I knew very well that if I omitted the appointment of the gentleman, it would be heralded throughout the length and breadth of the country, by the *claquers* who have so industriously distributed this letter this morning, that the Speaker had packed the committee, as the gentleman said he would, with "weak-kneed Republicans," who would not go into an investigation vigorously, as he would. That was the reason. [Applause] So that the Chair laid the responsibility upon the gentleman of declining the appointment.

Mr. Butler. I knew that was the trick of the Chair.

Mr. Blaine. Ah, the "trick!" We now know what the gentleman meant by the word "trick." I am very glad to know that the "trick" was successful.

Mr. Butler. No doubt.

Mr. Blaine. It is this "trick" which places the gentleman from Massachusetts on his responsibility before the country.

Mr. Butler. Exactly.

Mr. Blaine. Wholly.

Mr. Butler. Wholly.

Mr. Blaine. Now, sir, the gentleman from Massachusetts talks about the coercion by which fifty-eight Republicans were made to vote for the resolution. I do not know what any one of them may have to say; but if there be here to-day a single gentleman who has given to the gentleman of Massachusetts the intimation that he felt coerced—that he was in any way restrained from free action, let him get up now and speak, or "forever after hold his peace."

Mr. Butler. Oh, yes.

Mr. Blaine. The gentleman from Massachusetts says: "Having been appointed against my wishes, expressed both publicly and privately, by the Speaker, as chairman of a committee to investigate the state of affairs in the South, ordered to-day by Democratic votes, against the most earnest protest of *more than a two-thirds majority* of the Republicans of the House."

Mr. Butler. Yes, sir.

Mr. Blaine. This statement is so bold and groundless that I do not know what reply to make to it. It is made in the face of the fact that on the roll-call fifty-eight Republicans voted for the resolution, and forty-nine, besides the gentleman from Massachusetts, against it. I deny that the gentleman has the right to speak for any member who voted for it, unless it may be the gentleman from Tennessee (Mr. Maynard), who voted for it, for the purpose, probably, of moving a reconsideration—a very common, a very justifiable and proper course whenever any gentleman chooses to adopt it. I am not criticising it at all. But if there be any one of the fifty-eight gentlemen who voted for the resolution under coercion I would like the gentleman from Massachusetts to designate him.

Mr. Butler. I am not here to retail private conversations.

Mr. Blaine. Oh, no; but you will distribute throughout the entire country unfounded calumnies purporting to rest upon assertions made in private conversations, which, when called for, cannot be verified.

Mr. Butler. Pardon me, sir. I said there was a caucus ——

Mr. Blaine. I hope God will pardon you; but you ought not to ask me to do it! [Laughter.]

Mr. Butler. I will ask God, and not you.

Mr. Blaine. I am glad the gentleman will.

Mr. Butler. I have no favors to ask of the devil. And let me say that the caucus agreed upon a definite mode of action.

Mr. Blaine. The caucus! Now, let me say here, and now that the Chairman of that caucus, sitting on my right, "a chevalier," in legislation, "sans peur et sans reproche," the gentleman from Michigan (Mr. Austin Blair) stated, as a man of honor, as he is, that he was bound to say officially from the Chair that it was not considered, and could not be considered binding upon gentlemen. And more than that. Talk about tricks! Why, the very infamy of political trickery never compassed a design so foolish and so wicked as to bring together a caucus, and attempt to pledge them to the support of measures which might violate not only the political principles, but the religious faith of men—to the support of the bill drawn by the gentleman from Massachusetts, which might violate the conscientious scruples of men. And yet, forsooth, he comes in here and declares that whatever a caucus may determine upon, however hastily, however crudely, however wrongfully, you must support it! Why, even in the worst days of the Democracy, when the gentleman himself was in the front rank of the worst wing of it, when was it ever attempted to say that a majority of a party caucus could bind men upon measures that involved questions of constitutional law, of personal honor, of religious scruple? The gentleman asked what would have been done— he asked my colleague (Mr. Peters) what would have been done in case of members of a party voting against the caucus nominee for Speaker. I understand that was intended as a thrust at myself. Caucus nominations of officers have always been held as binding. But, just here, let me say, that if a minority did not vote against the decision of the caucus that nominated me for Speaker, in my judgment, it was not the fault of the gentleman from Massachusetts. [Applause.] If the requisite number could have been found to have gone over to the despised Nazarenes on the opposite side, that gentleman would have led them as gallantly as he did the forces in the Charleston Convention. [Renewed applause and laughter.]

Mr. Speaker, in old times it was the ordinary habit of the Speaker of the House of Representatives to take part in debate. The custom has fallen into disuse. For one, I am very glad that it has. For one, I approve of the conclusion that forbids it. The Speaker should, with consistent fidelity to his own party, be the impartial administrator of the rules of the House, and a constant participation in the discussions of members would take from him that appearance of impartiality which it is so important to maintain in the rulings of the Chair. But at the same time I despise and denounce the insolence of the gentleman from Massachusetts when he attempts to say that the Representative from the Third District of the State of Maine has no right to frame a resolution; has no right to seek that under the rules that resolutions shall be adopted; has no right to ask the judgment of the House upon that resolution. Why, even the insolence of the gentleman himself never reached that sublime height before.

*   *   *   *   *   *   *   *   *   *

Now, Mr. Speaker, nobody regrets more sincerely than I do any occurrence which calls me to take the floor. On questions of propriety, I appeal to members on both sides of the House, and they will bear me witness, that the circulation of this letter in the morning prints; its distribution throughout the land by telegraph; the laying it upon the desks of members, was intended to be by the gentleman from Massachusetts, not openly and boldly, but covertly—I will not use a stronger phrase—an insult to the Speaker of this House. As such I resent it. I denounce it in all its essential statements, and in all its misstatements, and in all its mean inferences and meaner innuendoes. I denounce the letter as groundless without justification; and the gentleman himself, I trust, will live to see the day when he will be ashamed of having written it.

[From Congressional Record for Second Session of Forty-second Congress, page 4461.]

When the Second Session of the Forty-second Congress adjourned finally, on the 8th day of June, 1872, Mr. Niblack, of Indiana, took the Chair temporarily,

when Mr. Samuel J. Randall, of Pennsylvania, submitted the following resolution :

Resolved, That the thanks of this House are due,
and are hereby tendered to James G. Blaine, Speaker
of the House, for the able, prompt and impartial
manner in which he has discharged the duties of his
office during the present session.

The resolution was unanimously adopted.

During the Presidential campaign of 1872, charges
of bribery were preferred against a number of men
occupying high and honored positions in the public
service.   This induced Mr. Blaine to take the floor in
the House when Congress convened in regular session
on the 2d day of December, 1872, when he addressed
the House as follows :

[Mr. Cox, of New York, in the Chair.]

Mr. Speaker, I rise to a question of the highest
privilege, to one that concerns the integrity of members of this House and the honor of the House itself.
It is quite generally known to the members of this
House that during the recent Presidential campaign
there was a wide-spread accusation of bribery of
members; that members of this House were bribed to
perform certain legislative acts for the benefit of the
Union Pacific Railroad Company, by presents of
stock in a corporation known as the "Credit Mobilier."
Without obtruding myself as one of eminent station,
I may say that the charge struck in high places.   It
included the Vice-President of the United States ; the
Vice-President-elect of the United States; it included
three Senators of the United States—two of them
ex-Senators from Tennessee and Delaware, and one a
present Senator from New Hampshire; it included

the Secretary of the Treasury of the United States;
it included honorable and prominent members of this
House—my friend, the Chairman of the Ways and
Means (Mr. Dawes); my friend, the Chairman of the
Appropriations Committee (Mr. Garfield); the gen-
tleman from Pennsylvania (Mr. Kelley), the Chairman
of the Civil-Service Committee: the gentleman from
Ohio (Mr. Bingham), the Chairman of the Judiciary
Committee; the gentleman from Pennsylvania (Mr.
Schofield), the Chairman of the Naval Committee.
On the other side of the House, the prominent and
distinguished member of the Ways and Means Committee from New York (Mr. Brooks); and a member
from Pennsylvania (Mr. Boyer), not now in this
House; and besides these a gentleman from Massachusetts (Mr. Eliot), no longer among the living, but
sleeping in what was considered an honored grave.
These accusations are that the several persons received bribes from the hands of a Representative
from Massachusetts (Mr. Ames). A charge of bribery
of members is the gravest that can be made in a
legislative body. It seems to me, sir, that this charge
demands prompt, thorough and impartial investigation, and I have taken the floor for the purpose of
moving that investigation. Unwilling, of course, to
appoint any committee of investigation to examine
into a charge in which I was myself included, I have
called you, sir, to the Chair, an honored member of
the House, honored here and honored in the country;
and when on Saturday last I called upon you and advised you of this service, I placed upon you no other
restriction in the appointment of a committee than
that it should not contain a majority of my political
friends.

I therefore send to the **Clerk's desk,** for adoption by the **House, a** preamble and **accompanying resolution.**

It was read by the Clerk as follows :

WHEREAS accusations **have been made in the public** press, founded on the alleged letters of OAKES AMES, a **Representative from** Massachusetts, **and upon the alleged affidavit of Henry C. McComb, a citizen of Wilmington, in the State of Delaware, to the effect that members of this House were bribed by** OAKES AMES **to perform certain legislative acts for the benefit of** the **Union Pacific Railway Company, by** presents **of stock in the Credit Mobilier of** America, or by presents **of a valuable character derived therefrom;** therefore,

Resolved, **That a special committee of five members be appointed by the Speaker** *pro tempore,* **whose duty it shall be to investigate and ascertain whether any member of this House was bribed by** OAKES AMES **in any matter touching his legislative duty.**

Resolved further, **That the committee** have the right **to employ a** stenographer, **and that they be empowered to send for persons and papers.**

The resolution was agreed to.

On the 3d of March, 1873, Mr. Voorhees of Indiana spoke as **follows :**

[**Hon. W**m. A. **Wheeler, of New** York, in the Chair.] I **rise to** present a matter to the House in which I am sure every member will concur. In doing **so I** perform the most pleasant duty of **my** entire service **on** this floor. I offer the following resolution. It has the sincere sanction of **my** head and of my heart. I **move its adoption.**

The Clerk read as follows :

Resolved, That the thanks of this House are due, and are hereby tendered, to Hon. James G. Blaine, for the distinguished ability and impartiality with which he has discharged the duty of Speaker of the House of Representatives of the Forty-second Congress.

The resolution was adopted unanimously.

On the same day, in adjourning the House *sine die*, Mr. Blaine spoke as follows :

Gentlemen: For the forty-second time since the Federal Government was organized, its great representative body stands on the eve of dissolution. The final word which separates us is suspended for a moment that I may return my sincere thanks for the kind expressions respecting my official conduct,which, without division of party, you have caused to be entered on your journal.

At the close of four years service in this responsible and often trying position, it is a source of honorable pride that I have so administered my trust as to secure the confidence and approbation of both sides of the House. It would not be strange if, in the necessarily rapid discharge of the daily business, I should have erred in some of the decisions made on points, and often without precedent to guide me. It has been my good fortune, however, to be always sustained by the House, and in no single instance to have had a ruling reversed. I advert to this gratifying fact, to quote the language of the most eloquent of my predecessors, " in no vain spirit of exhaltation, but as furnishing a powerful motive for undissembled gratitude."

And now, gentlemen, with a hearty God bless you all, I discharge my only remaining duty in declaring that the House of Representatives for the Forty-second Congress is adjourned without day. [Applause.]

On the 2nd day of December, 1873, Hon. James G. Blaine, of Maine, was chosen Speaker of the United States House of Representatives for the third time, Mr. Blaine receiving 189 votes to 80 votes cast for all others. After being conducted to the chair by Mr. Maynard, of Tennessee, and Mr. Wood, of New York, he addressed the House as follows :

Gentlemen of the House of Representatives: The vote this moment announced by the Clerk, is such an expression of your confidence as calls for my sincerest thanks. To be chosen Speaker of the American House of Representatives is always an honorable distinction ; to be chosen a third time enhances the honor more than three-fold ; to be chosen by the largest body that ever assembled in the Capitol imposes a burden of responsibility which only your indulgent kindness could embolden me to assume.

The first occupant of this Chair presided over a House of sixty-five members representing a population far below the present aggregate of the State of New York. At that time in the whole United States there were not fifty thousand civilized inhabitants to be found one hundred miles distant from the flow of the Atlantic tide. To-day, gentlemen, a large body of you come from beyond that limit, and represent districts then peopled only by the Indian and adventurous frontiersman. The National Government is not yet as old as many of its citizens ; but in this brief span of time, less than one lengthened life, it has, under God's providence, extended its power until a continent is the field of its empire and attests the majesty of its law.

With the growth of new States and the resulting changes in the centers of population, new interests are developed, rival to the old, but by no means hostile, diverse but not antagonistic. Nay, rather are all these interests in harmony; and the true science of just government is to give to each its full and fair play, oppressing none by undue exaction, favoring none by undue privilege. It is this great lesson which our daily experience is teaching us, binding us together more closely, making our mutual dependence more manifest, and causing us to feel, whether we live in the North or in the South, in the East or in the West, that we have indeed but "one country, one Constitution, one destiny."

The oath of office was then administered by Henry L. Dawes, of Massachusetts, the oldest member in continuous service.

Upon the occasion of a reception given by the United States Senate and House of Representatives on the 18th of December, 1874, to the King of the Hawaiian Islands, after the Senators had filed into the Hall of the House, and had taken seats assigned them to the Speaker's right, and the joint committee of reception had escorted the Hawaiian King, attended by his suite down the main aisle fronting the Speaker, the latter addressed His majesty, thus:

Your Majesty : On behalf of the American Congress I welcome you to these Halls. The Senators from our States and the Representatives of our people unite in cordial congratulations upon your auspicious journey, and in the expression of the gratification and pleasure afforded by your presence in the Capitol of the nation as the nation's guest.

Your Majesty's appearance among us is the first instance in which a reigning sovereign has set foot upon the soil of the United States, and it is a significant circumstance that the visit comes to us from the West and not from the East. Probably no single event could more strikingly typify the century's progress in your Majesty's country and in our own than the scene here and now transpiring.

The rapid growth of the Republic on its Western coast has greatly enlarged our intercourse with your insular kingdom, and has led us all to a knowledge of your wisdom and beneficence as a ruler, and your exalted virtues as a man. Our whole people cherish for your subjects the most friendly regard. They trust and believe that the relations of the two countries will always be as peaceful as the great sea that rolls between us—uniting and not dividing!

Chief Justice Allen of the Hawaiian Islands responded in behalf of the King.

At the expiration of the Forty-third Congress on the 3d day of March, 1875, Mr. Potter submitted the following resolution :

Resolved, That the thanks of this House are due, and are hereby tendered, to Hon. James G. Blaine, Speaker of the House of Representatives, for the impartiality, efficiency and distinguished ability with which he has discharged the trying and arduous duties of his office during the Forty-third Congress.

The resolution was unanimously agreed to.

On the same day, when the clock indicated that the hour for the dissolution of the Forty-third Congress had arrived, Speaker Blaine delivered the following valedictory address:

Gentlemen: I close with this hour a six years' service as Speaker of the House of Representatives —a period surpassed in length by but two of my predecessors, and equaled by only two others. The rapid mutations of personal and political fortunes in this country have limited the great majority of those who have occupied this Chair to shorter terms of office.

It would be the gravest insensibility to the honors and responsibilities of life, not to be deeply touched by so signal a mark of public esteem as that which I have thrice received at the hands of my political associates. I desire in this last moment to renew to them, one and all, my thanks and my gratitude.

To those from whom I differ in my party relations—the minority of this House—I tender my acknowledgements for the generous courtesy with which they have treated me. By one of those sudden and decisive changes which distinguish popular institutions, and which conspicuously mark a free people, that minority is transformed in the ensuing Congress to the governing power of the House. However it might possibly have been under other circumstances, that event renders these words my farewell to the Chair.

The Speakership of the American House of Representatives is a post of honor, of dignity, of power, of responsibility. Its duties are at once complex and continuous; they are both onerous and delicate; they are performed in the broad light of day, under the eye of the whole people, subject at all times to the closest observation, and always attended with the sharpest criticism. I think no other official is held to such instant and such rigid accountability. Parliamentary rulings in their very nature are peremptory: almost absolute in authority and instantaneous in effect. They cannot always be enforced in such a way as to win applause or secure popularity; but I am sure that no man of any party who is worthy to fill this chair will ever see a dividing line between duty and policy.

Thanking you once more, and thanking you most cordially for the honorable testimonial you have placed on record to my credit, I perform my only remaining duty in declaring that the Forty-third Congress has reached its constitutional limit, and that the House of Representatives stands adjourned without day. [Great applause all over the hall.]

It has often been said that no man since Clay's Speakership presided with such an absolute knowledge of the rules of the House, or with so great a mastery in the rapid, intelligent, and faithful discharge of business as Mr. Blaine. His knowledge of parliamentary law was instinctive and complete, and his administration of it so fair that both sides of the House, as we have seen, at the close of each Congress, united in cordial thanks for his impartiality. As Mr. Blaine presided over some of the most exciting scenes and sessions of the House, the approval he secured is especially noticeable.

AGAIN ON THE FLOOR OF THE HOUSE.

The Forty-fourth Congress—which was elected in the Democratic "tidal wave" of 1874, and which met

4

December 6, 1875— had a large Democratic majority, and elected Michael C. Kerr, of Indiana, Speaker. Mr. Blaine took his place on the floor of the House as the recognized leader of the Republican minority. In a sudden tilt, in a day, by his aggressive and un-expected tactics, he changed a victorious and exultant Democratic majority into a surprised, subdued and saddened crowd. The debates of that memorable ses-sion on the proposition to remove the disabilities of Jefferson Davis are still fresh in people's minds. The excitements growing out of that exciting session brought Mr. Blaine more prominently before the country than any other citizen of the time, centered upon him a hostility more malignant and a love far more enthusiastic than are often inspired by public service. The following are the most important of Mr. Blaine's speeches during that eventful session of Congress:

On January, 10, 1876, Mr. Blaine spoke on the Amnesty bill as follows:

The House having under consideration the bill (H. R. 214) to remove the disabilities imposed by the Third Section of the Fourteenth Article of the Amend-ment of the Constitution of the United States, the pending question being on the motion of Mr. Blaine to reconsider the motion by which the bill was repealed.

MR. BLAINE: *Mr. Speaker*, I rise to a privileged question. I move to reconsider the vote which has just been declared. I propose to debate that motion, and now give notice that, if the motion to reconsider is agreed to, it is my intention to offer the amendment which has been read several times. I will not delay the House to have it read again.

Every time the question of amnesty has been brought before the House, by a gentleman on that side for the last two Congresses, it has been done with a certain flourish of magnanimity which is an imputation on this side of the House, as though the Republican party which has been in charge of the Government for the last twelve or fourteen years had been bigoted, narrow, and illiberal, and as though certain very worthy and deserving gentlemen in the Souhtern States were ground down to-day under a great tyranny and oppression, from which the hard-heartedness of this side of the House cannot possibly be prevailed upon to relieve them.

If I may anticipate as much wisdom as ought to characterize that side of the House, this may be the last time that amnesty will be discussed in the American Congress. I therefore desire, and under the rules of the House, with no thanks to that side for the privilege, to place on record just what the Republican party has done in this matter. I wish to place it there as an imperishable record of liberality and large-mindedness, and magnanimity, and mercy far beyond any that has ever been shown before in the world's history by conqueror to conquered.

With the gentleman from Pennsylvania, (Mr. RANDALL) I entered Congress in the midst of the hot flame of war, when the Union was rocking to its foundations, and no man knew whether we were to have a country or not. I think the gentleman from Pennsylvania would have been surprised, when he and I were novices in the Thirty-eighth Congress, if he could have foreseen before our joint service ended, we should have seen sixty-one gentlemen, then in arms against us, admitted to equal privileges with ourselves, and all by the grace and magnanimity of the Republican party. When the war ended, according to the universal usages of nations, the Government, then under the exclusive control of the Republican party, had the right to determine what should be the political status of the people who had been defeated in war. Did we inaugurate any measures of persecution? Did we set forth on a career of bloodshed and vengeance? Did we take property? Did we prohibit any man all his civil rights? Did we take away from him the right he enjoys to-day to vote?

Not at all. But instead of a general and sweeping condemnation the Republican party placed in the Fourteenth Amendment to the Constitution only this exclusion; after considering the whole subject it ended it, simply coming down to this:

That no person shall be a Senator or Representative in Congress, or Elector of President or Vice-President, or hold any office, civil or military, under the United States or under any State, who, having previously taken an oath as a member of Congress, or as an officer of the United States, or as a member of any State Legislature, or as an executive or judicial officer of any State, to support the Constitution of the United States shall have engaged in insurrection or rebellion against the same, or given aid or comfort to the enemies thereof. But Congress may, by a vote of two-thirds of each House, remove such disability.

It has been variously estimated that this Section at the time of its original insertion in the Constitution included somewhere from fourteen to thirty thousand persons; as nearly as I can gather together the facts of the case, it included about eighteen thousand men in the South. It let go every man of the hundreds of thousands—or millions, if you please—who had

been engaged in the attempt to destroy this Government, and only held those under disability who in addition to revolting had violated a special and peculiar
and personal oath to support the Constitution of the
United States.   It was limited to that.

Well, that disability was hardly placed upon the
South until we began in this hall and in the other
wing of the Capitol, when there were more than two-
thirds Republicans in both branches, to remit it, and
the very first bill took that disability off from 1,578
citizens of the South ; and the next bill took it off
from 3,526 gentlemen—by wholesale.   Many of the
gentlemen on this floor came in for grace and amnesty
in those two bills.   After these bills specifying individuals had passed, and others, of smaller numbers,
which I will not recount, the Congress of the United
States in 1872, by two-thirds of both branches, still
being two-thirds Republican, passed this general law:

That all political disabilities imposed by the Third
Section of the Fourteenth Article of Amendments of
the Constitution of the United States are hereby removed ·from all persons whomsoever, except Senators
and Representatives of the Thirty-sixth and Thirty-
seventh Congresses, officers in the judicial, military,
and naval service of the United States, heads of departments, and foreign ministers of the United
States.

Since that act passed a very considerable number
of the gentlemen which are still left under disability
have been relieved specially, by name, in separate
acts.   But I believe, Mr. Speaker, in no single instance since the Act of May 22, 1872, have the disabilities been taken from any man except upon his
respectful petition to the Congress of the United
States that they should be removed.   And I believe

in no instance, except one, have they been refused upon the petition being presented. I believe in no instance, except one, has there been any other than a unanimous vote.

Now, I find there are widely varying opinions in regard to the number that are still under disabilities in the South.

I have had occasion, by conference with the Departments of War and of the Navy, and with the assistance of some records which I have caused to be searched, to be able to state to the House, I believe, with more accuracy than it has been stated hitherto, just the number of gentlemen in the South still under disabilities. Those who were officers of the United States Army, educated at its own expense at West Point, and who joined the rebellion, and are still included under this Act, number, as nearly as the War Department can figure it up. 325: those in the Navy about 295. Those under the other heads, Senators and Representatives of the Thirty-sixth and Thirty-seventh Congresses, officers in the judiciary service of the United States, heads of departments, and foreign ministers of the United States, make up a number somewhat more difficult to state accurately, but smaller in the aggregate. The whole sum of the entire list is about—it is probably impossible to state it with entire accuracy, and I do not attempt to do that—is about 750 persons now under disabilities.

I am very frank to say that in regard to all these gentlemen, save one, I do not know of any reason why amnesty should not be granted to them as it has been to many others of the same class. I am not here to argue against it. The gentlemen from Iowa (MR. KASSON) suggests "on their application." I am coming to that.   But as I have said, seeing in this list, as I have examined it with some care, no gentleman to whom I think there would be any objection, since amnesty has already become so general—and I am not going back of that question to argue it—I am in favor of granting it them.   But in the absence of this respectful form of application, which, since May 22, 1872, has become a sort of common law as preliminary to amnesty, I simply wish to put in that they shall go before a United States Court, and in open court, with uplifted hand, swear that they mean to conduct themselves as good citizens of the United States.   That is all.

Now, gentlemen may say that this is a foolish exaction.   Possibly it is.   But, somehow or other, I have a prejudice in favor of it.   And there are some pretty points in it that appeal as well to prejudice as to conviction.   For one, I do not want to impose citizenship on any gentleman.   If I am correctly informed, and I state it only on rumor, there are some gentlemen in this list who have spoken contemptuously of the idea of their taking citizenship, and have spoken still more contemptuously of the idea of their applying for citizenship.   I may state it wrongly, and if I do I am willing to be corrected; but I understand that Mr. Robert Toombs has, on several occasions, at watering places both in this country and in Europe, stated that he would not ask the United States for citizenship.

Very well, we can stand it about as well as Mr. Robert Toombs can.   And if Mr. Robert Toombs is not prepared to go into court of the United States and swear that he means to be a good citizen, let him stay out.   I do not think that the two Houses of

Congress should convert themselves into a joint convention for the purpose of embracing Mr. Robert Toombs and gushingly request him to favor us by coming back to accept of all the honors of citizenship. That is the whole. All I ask is that each of these gentlemen shall show his good faith by coming forward and taking the oath which you on that side of the House, and we on this side of the House, and all of us take, and gladly take. It is a very small exaction to make as a preliminary to a full restoration to all the rights of citizenship.

In my amendment, Mr. Speaker, I have excepted Jefferson Davis from its operation. Now I do not place it on the ground that Mr. Davis was, as he has been commonly called, the head and front of the rebellion, because on that ground I do not think the exception would be tenable. Mr. Davis was just as guilty, no more so, no less so, than thousands of others, who have already received the benefit and grace of amnesty. Probably he was far less efficient as an enemy of the United States; probably he was far more useful as a disturber of the councils of the Confederacy than many who have already received amnesty. It is not because of any particular and special damage that he above others did to the Union, or because he was personally or especially of consequence, that I except him. But I except him on this ground: that he was the author, knowingly, deliberately, guiltily, and willfully, of the gigantic murders and crimes at Andersonville.

A MEMBER. And Libby.

MR. BLAINE. Libby pales into insignificance before Andersonville. I place it on that ground, and I believe to-day, that so rapidly does one event follow on the heels of another in the rapid age in which we live, that even those of us who were contemporaneous with what was transpiring there, and still less those who have grown up since, fail to remember the gigantic crime then committed.

Sir, since the gentleman from Pennsylvania (Mr. Randall) introduced this bill last month, I have taken occasion to re-read some of the historic cruelties of the world.

I have read over the details of those atrocious murders of the Duke of Alva in the Low Countries, which are always mentioned with a thrill of horror throughout Christendom. I have read the details of the massacre of Saint Bartholomew, that stand out in history as one of those atrocities beyond imagination. I have read anew the horrors untold and unimaginable of the Spanish Inquisition. And I here before God, measuring my words, knowing their full extent and import, declare that neither the deeds of the Duke of Alva in the Low Countries, nor the massacre of Saint Bartholomew, nor the thumb-screws and engines of torture of the Spanish Inquisition begin to compare in atrocity with the hideous crime of Andersonville. [Applause on the floor and in the galleries].

MR. ROBBINS, of North Carolina. That is an infamous slander.

The SPEAKER. If such demonstrations are repeated in the galleries the Chair will order them to be cleared.

MR. BLAINE. Thank God, Mr. Speaker, that while this Congress was under different control from that which exists here to-day, with a committee composed of both sides and of both branches, that tale of horror was placed where it cannot be denied or gainsaid.

I hold in my hand the story written out by a committee of Congress. I state that Winder who is dead, was sent to Andersonville with a full knowledge of his previous atrocities; that these atrocities in Richmond were so fearful, so terrible, that Confederate papers, the Richmond *Examiner* for one, stated when he was gone that, "Thank God, Richmond is rid of his presence." We in the North knew from returning skeletons what he had accomplished at Belle Isle and Libby, and fresh from those accomplishments he was sent by Mr. Davis, against the protest of others in the Confederacy, to construct this den of horrors at Andersonville.

Now, of course, it would be utterly beyond the scope of the occasion and beyond the limits of my hour for me to go into details. But in arraigning Mr. Davis I undertake here to say that I will not ask any gentleman to take the testimony of a single Union soldier. I ask them to take only the testimony of men who themselves were engaged and enlisted in the Confederate cause. And if that testimony does not entirely carry out and justify the declaration I have made, then I will state that I have been entirely in error in my reading.

After detailing the preparation of that prison, the arrangements made with hideous cruelty for the victims, the report which I hold in my hand, and which was concurred in by Democratic members as well as Republican members of Congress, states this—and I beg members to hear it, for it is far more impressive than anything I can say. After, I say, giving full details, the report states:

The subsequent history of Andersonville has startled and shocked the world with a tale of horror,

of woe, and death before unheard and unknown to
civilization.   No pen can describe, no painter sketch,
no imagination comprehend its fearful and unutterable
iniquity.   It would seem as if the concentrated madness of earth and hell had found its final lodgment in
the breast of those who inaugurated the rebellion and
controlled the policy of the Confederate Government,
and that the prison at Andersonville had been selected
for the most terrible human sacrifice which the world
has ever seen.   Into its narrow walls were crowded
thirty-five thousand enlisted men, many of them the
bravest and best, the most devoted and heroic of those
grand armies which carried the flag of their country to
final victory.   For long and weary months here they
suffered, maddened, were murdered and died.   Here
they lingered, unsheltered from the burning rays of
a tropical sun by day, and drenching and deadly dews
by night, in every stage of mental and physical disease, hungered, emaciated, starving, maddened; fes-
tering with unhealed wounds; gnawed by the rav-
ages of scurvy and gangrene; with swollen limb and
distorted visage; covered with vermin which they
had no power to extirpate; exposed to the flooding
rains which drove them drowning from the miserable
holes in which, like swine, they burrowed; parched
with thirst and mad with hunger; racked with pain
or prostrated with the weakness of dissolution; with
naked limbs and matted hair; filthy with smoke and
mud; soiled with the very excrement from which
their weakness would not permit them to escape;
eaten by the gnawing worms which their own wounds
had engendered; with no bed but the earth; no covering save the cloud or the sky; these men, these heroes, born in the image of God, thus crouching and
writhing in their terrible torture and calculating bar-
barity, stand forth in history as a monument of the
surpassing horrors of Andersonville as it shall be
seen and read in all future time, realizing in the
studied torments of their prison-house the ideal of
Dante's Inferno and Milton's Hell.

     I undertake to say, from reading the testimony,

that that is a moderate description. I will read but a single paragraph from the testimony of Rev. William John Hamilton, a man I believe who never was in the North, a Catholic priest at Macon. He is a Southern man, and a Democrat, and a Catholic priest. And when you unite those three qualities in one man you will not find much testimony that would be strained in favor of the Republican party. [Laughter.]

This man had gone to Andersonville on a mission of mercy to the men of his own faith, to administer to them the rights of his church in their last moments. That is why he happened to be a witness. I will read his answer under oath to a question addressed to him in regard to the bodily condition of the prisoners. He said :

Well, as I said before, when I went there I was kept so busily engaged in giving the sacrament to the dying men that I could not observe much ; but of course I could not keep my eyes closed as to what I saw here. I saw a great many men perfectly naked—

[Their clothes had been taken away from them as other testimony shows.]

walking about the stockade perfectly nude ; they seemed to have lost all regard for delicacy, shame, morality, or anything else. I would frequently have to creep on my hands and knees into the holes that the men had burrowed in the ground, and stretch myself out alongside of them to hear their confessions. I found them almost living in vermin in those holes ; they could not be in any other condition but a filthy one because they got no soap and no change of clothing, and were there all huddled up together.

Let me read further from the same witness another specimen :

The first person I conversed with on entering the stockade was a countryman of mine, a member of the

Catholic Church, who recognized me as a clergyman.
I think his name was Farrell. He was from the North
of Ireland. He came towards me and introduced
himself. He was quite a boy; I do not think, judg-
ing from his appearance, that he could have been
more than sixteen years old. I found him without
a hat and without any covering on his feet, and without jacket or coat. He told me that his shoes had been
taken from him on the battle-field. I found the boy
suffering very much from a wound on his right foot;
in fact the foot was split open like an oyster; and on
inquiring the cause they told me it was from exposure
to the sun in the stockade, and not from any wound
received in battle. I took off my boots and gave him
a pair of socks to cover his feet and told him I would
bring him some clothing, as I expected to return to
Andersonville the following week. I had to return to
Macon to get another priest to take my place on
Sunday. When I returned on the following week, on
inquiring for this man Farrell, his companions told
me he had stepped across the dead-line and requested
the guards to shoot him. He was not insane at the
time I was conversing with him.

Now, Mr. Speaker, I do not desire to go into such
horrible details as these for any purpose of arousing
bad feeling. I wish only to say that the man who
administered the affairs of that prison went there by
order of Mr. Davis, was sustained by him; and this
William John Hamilton, from whose testimony I
have read, states here that he went to General Howell
Cobb, commanding that department, and asked that
intelligence as to the condition of affairs there be
transmitted to the Confederate Government at Richmond. For the matter of that, there are a great
many proofs to show that Mr. Davis was thoroughly
informed as to the condition of affairs at Andersonville.

One word more, and I shall lay aside this book.

When the march of General Sherman, or some other invasion of that portion of the country, was under way, there was danger, or supposed danger, that it might come into the neighborhood of Andersonville; and the following order—to which I invite the attention of the House—a regular military order—order No. 13, dated Headquarters Confederate States military prison, Andersonville, July 27, 1864, was issued by Brigadier-General John H. Winder:

The officers on duty and in charge of the battery of Florida artillery at the time, will, upon receiving notice that the enemy have approached within seven miles of this post, *open fire upon the stockade with grape-shot* without reference to the situation beyond these lines of defense.

Now, here were these 35,000 poor, helpless, naked, starving, sickened, dying men. This Catholic priest states that he begged Mr. Cobb to represent that if they could not exchange those men. or could not relieve them in any other way, they should be taken to the Union lines in Florida and paroled; for they were shadows, they were skeletons. Yet it was declared by a regular order of Mr. Davis' officer, that if the Union forces should come within seven miles the battery of Florida artillery should open fire with grape-shot on these poor, helpless men, without the slightest possible regard to what was going on outside.

Now I do not arraign the Southern people for this. God forbid that I should charge any people with sympathizing with such things. There were many evidences of great uneasiness among the Southern people about it; and one of the great crimes of Jefferson Davis was, that besides conniving at and producing that condition of things, he concealed it from the Southern people. He labored not only to conceal it, but to make false statements about it. We have obtained, and have now in the Congressional Library, a complete series of Mr. Davis' messages—the official imprint from Richmond. I have looked over them, and I have here an extract from his message of November 7, 1864. at the very time that these horrors were at their acme. Mark you, when those horrors of which I have read specimens were at their extremest verge of desperation, Mr. Davis sends a message to the Confederate Congress at Richmond, in which he says :

The solicitude of the Government for the relief of our captive fellow citizens has known no abatement, but has on the contrary been still more deeply evoked by the additional sufferings to which they have been wantonly subjected by deprivation of adequate food, clothing, and fuel, which they were not even permitted to purchase from the prison sutler.

And he adds that—

The enemy attempted to excuse their barbarous treatment by the unfounded allegation that it was retaliatory for like conduct on our part.

Now I undertake here to say that there is not a Confederate soldier now living who has any credit as a man in his community, and who ever was a prisoner in the hands of the Union forces, who will say that he ever was cruelly treated ; and that he ever was deprived of the same rations that the Union soldiers had—the same food and the same clothing.

Mr. COOK. .Thousands of them say it—thousands of them ; men of as high character as any in this House.

Mr. BLAINE. I take issue upon that. There is

not one who can substantiate it—not one. As for
measures of retaliation, although goaded by this
terrific treatment of our friends imprisoned by Mr.
Davis, the Senate of the United States specifically
refused to pass a resolution of retaliation, as contrary to modern civilization and the first precepts of
Christianity. And there was no retaliation attempted
or justified. It was refused; and Mr. Davis knew it
was refused just as well as I knew it or any other
man, because what took place in Washington or what
took place at Richmond was known on either side of
the line within a day or two thereafter.

Mr. Speaker, this is *not a proposition to punish
Jefferson Davis.* There is nobody attempting that.
I will very frankly say that I myself thought the
indictment of Mr. Davis at Richmond, under the
Administration of Mr. Johnson, was a weak attempt,
for he was indicted only for that of which he was
guilty in common with all others who went into the
Confederate movement. Therefore, there was no particular reason for it. But I will undertake to say
this, and, as it may be considered an extreme speech,
I want to say it with great deliberation, that there is
not a government, a civilized government, on the face
of the globe—I am very sure there is not a European
government—that would not have arrested Mr. Davis,
and when they had him in their power would not have
tried him for maltreatment of the prisoners of war
and shot him within thirty days. France, Russia, England. Germany, Austria, any one of them would have
done it. The poor victim, Wirz, deserved his death
for brutal treatment and murder of many victims, but
I always thought it was a weak movement on the
part of our Government to allow Jefferson Davis to

go at large and hang Wirz. I confess I do. Wirz was nothing in the world but a mere subordinate, a tool, and there was no special reason for singling him out for death. I do not say he did not deserve it—he did, richly, amply, fully. He deserved no mercy, but at the same time, as I have often said, it seemed like skipping over the President, Superintendent. and Board of Directors, in the case of a great railroad accident, and hanging the brakeman of the rear car. [Laughter.]

There is no proposition here to punish Jefferson Davis. Nobody is seeking to do it. That time has gone by. The statute of limitations, common feelings of humanity, will supervene for his benefit. But what you ask us to do is to declare, by a vote of two-thirds of both branches of Congress, that we consider Mr. Davis worthy to fill the highest offices in the United States, if he can get a constituency to endorse him. He is a voter; he can buy and he can sell; he can go and he can come. He is as free as any man in the United States. There is a large list of subordinate offices to which he is eligible. This bill proposes, in view of that record, that Mr. Davis, by a two-thirds vote of the Senate and a two-thirds vote of the House, be declared eligible and worthy to fill any office up to the Presidency of the United States. For one, upon full deliberation, I will not do it.

One word more, Mr. Speaker, in the way of detail, which I omitted. It has often been said in mitigation of Jefferson Davis, in the Andersonville matter, that the men who died there in such large numbers (I think the victims were about fifteen thousand) fell prey to an epidemic, and died of a disease which could not be averted. The record shows that out of thirty-five thousand men about thirty-three per cent. died, that

5

is one in three, while of the soldiers encamped near
by to take care and guard them only one man in four
hundred died; that is, within half-a-mile, only one in
four hundred died.

As to the general question of amnesty, Mr. Speaker,
as I have already said, it is too late to debate it.   It
has gone by.   Whether it has in all respects been wise,
or whether it has been unwise, I would not detain the
House here to discuss.   Even if I had a strong conviction upon that question, I do not know that it
would be productive of any great good to enunciate
it; but, at the same time, it is a very singular spectacle that the Republican party, in possession of the
entire Government, have deliberately called back into
political power the leading men of the South, every
one of whom turns up its bitter and relentless and
malignant foe; and to-day, from the Potomac to the
Rio Grande, the very men who have received this
amnesty are as busy as they can be in consolidating
into one compact political organization the old slave
States, just as they were before the war.   We see the
banner held out blazoned again with the inscription
that with the United South and a very few votes from
the North this country can be governed.   I want the
people to understand that is precisely the movement;
and that is the animus and the intent.   I do not think
offering amnesty to the seven hundred and fifty men
who are now without it will hasten or retard that
movement.   I do not think the granting of amnesty
to Mr. Davis will hasten or retard it, or that refusing
it will do either.

I hear it said, "We will lift Mr. Davis again into great
consequence by refusing amnesty."   That is not for
me to consider; I only see before me, when his name

is presented, a man who by the wink of his eye, by a wave of his hand, by a nod of his head, could have stopped the atrocity at Andersonville.

Some of us had kinsmen there, most of us had friends there, all of us had countrymen there, and in the name of those kinsmen, friends, and countrymen, I here protest, and shall with my vote protest against their calling back and crowning with the honors of full American citizenship the man who organized that murder.

To this speech of Mr. Blaine's the Hon. Benjamin H. Hill, of Georgia, replied in lengthy speeches on the two following days (January 11 and 12, 1876).

On the 13th of January, Mr. Blaine replied to Mr. Hill's remarks.

The following is an extract from Mr. Blaine's remarks during the debate on the Amnesty Bill in the House of Representatives, January 13, 1876:

In connection with one point in history there is something which I should feel it my duty, not merely as a member of the Republican party which upheld the Administration that conducted the war, but as a citizen of the American Union, to resist and resent, and that is the allegations that were made in regard to the manner in which Confederate prisoners were treated in the prisons of the Union. The gentleman from Georgia said:

" I have also proved that with all the horrors you have made such a noise about as occurring at Andersonville, greater horrors occurred in the prisons where our troops were held."

And I could not but admire the "our" and "your" with which the gentleman conducted the whole discussion. It ill comported with his later professions of Unionism. It was certainly flinging the shadow of a dead Confederacy a long way over the dial of the National House of Representatives. And I think the gentleman from New York fell into a little of the same line. Of that I shall speak again. The gentleman from Georgia goes on to say that—

" The atrocities of Andersonville do not begin to compare with the atrocities of Elmira, of Camp Douglas. of Fort Delaware; and of all the atrocities both at Andersonville and Elmira the Confederate authorities stand acquitted."

MR. HILL. Will the gentleman allow me a moment?

MR. BLAINE. I yield for a moment.

MR. HILL. I certainly said no such thing. I stated distinctly that I brought no charge of crime against anybody. But I also stated distinctly that according to the gentleman's logic that result followed.

MR. BLAINE. But that is not the reported speech at all.

MR. HILL. I stated distinctly that I was following the gentleman's logic.

MR. BLAINE. I am quoting the gentleman's speech as he delivered it. I quote it as it appeared in the *Daily Chronicle* and the Associated Press report. I do not pretend to be bound by the version which may appear hereafter, because I observed that the gentleman from New York (Mr. Cox) spoke one speech and published another, [great laughter,] and I suppose the gentleman from Georgia (Mr. Hill) will do the same. I admit that the gentleman has a difficult *role* to play. He has to harmonize himself with the great Northern Democracy, and keep himself in high line as a Democratic candidate for Senator from Georgia, and it is a very difficult thing to reconcile the two. [Laughter.] The 'Barn-burner Democrats' in 1853 tried very hard to adhere to their anti-slavery principles in New York and still support the Pierce Administration; and Mr. Greeley, with that inimitable humor which he possessed, said that they found it very hard to straddle, like a militia general on parade on Broadway, who finds it an almost impossible task to follow the music and dodge the omnibuses. [Laughter.] And that is what the gentleman does. The gentleman tries to keep step to the music of the Union and dodge his fire-eating constituency in Georgia. [Great laughter.]

I confess—and I say it to the gentleman from Georgia (Mr. Hill) with no personal unkindness—I confess that my very blood boiled, if there was anything of tradition, of memory, of feeling, it boiled when I heard the gentleman, with his record which I have read, seconded and sustained by the gentleman from New York, arraigning the Administration of Abraham Lincoln, throwing obloquy and slander upon the grave of Edwin M. Stanton, and demanding that Jefferson Davis should be restored to full citizenship in this country. Ah! that is a novel spectacle; the gentleman from Georgia does not know how novel; the gentleman from New York ought to know. The gentleman from Georgia does not know, and he cannot know, how many hundred thousands of Northern bosoms were lacerated by his course.

These are Mr. Blaine's remarks on Riders on Appropriation Bills, in the House, March 21, 1876:

One of the evils that have come down to us from the experience of the British House of Commons, one that almost every State Legislature finds it neces-

sary to guard against, one that we are warned against
at the very threshold of our business here. is to keep
general legislation off your appropriation bills. Now,
the rule which the gentleman has put into our book
(which I have no doubt that in its motive it was just
as pure and equitable as it could be) opens the door
to all manner and measure of abuse. The gentleman
says that it was a considerable time before the old
rule bore its full fruit of evil. This new rule which
the gentleman has introduced may, like a new broom,
sweep clear for a time; but I tell him, with some
little experience in this matter—and he has even
more than I—that, unless I entirely mistake the
tendency and operation of rules of this kind, this
will ultimately open the door to immeasurable abuses
which the other was not competent to inflict. By
the operation of this rule, under the idea of retrench-
ing salaries, you may have all imaginable vicious legislation affecting the rights of the people, changing
radically the laws of the country, interfering with
every possible human right that may be reached by
Congressional enactment. Every conceivable measure of that kind may be piled upon an appropriation
bill; and under the thumb-screw, under the pressure
that attends legislation on appropriation bills, you thus
force through Congress what in its calmer moments,
upon the reports of appropriation committees, would
never even get a respectable hearing in this House.
In that view I think the rule is utterly vicious.

The following are remarks by Mr. Blaine on the Bill
"Making it a misdemeanor for any person in the em-
ploy of the United States to demand or contribute
Election Funds," in the House of Representatives,
March 21, 1876:

MR. BLAINE.   I have run seven times for Congress, and I never contributed so much as a postage stamp for any improper purpose in securing my election; but I could indicate gentlemen who, if rumor is to be trusted, have spent very large sums in political campaigns.

On the same bill, March 22, 1876:

MR. BLAINE.   It was very well remarked yesterday by the gentleman from Massachusetts (Mr. Hoar), that the worst form of government in the world to live under is a government of the people when the majority is bribed; and he stated very well that there was only one thing worse than the bribing of voters, and that was the fraudulent count of the votes after they were deposited in the ballot-box.

*   *   *   *   *   *   *   *   *   *

Bad as bribing the voter is, and it is an unendurable evil almost, it is not so bad as bold, naked fraud in the count.   There you have literally taken away the foundations of free government.   A fraud in the count is the destruction of Republican government. One or two men may do more there than a thousand bribed men can do outside.   *   *   *   This country demands elections shall be pure.   There is not an honest man in either party who does not desire it.   Without that all government is a failure; and, sir, there is a widespread conviction to-day that in a good many of the States of this Union it is impossible to get a fair election.   That the persons entitled to vote under the Fifteenth Amendment to the Constitution, the colored voters, get a fair show and equal chance to deposit their ballots is not believed by ten honest men North of Mason and Dixon's line, in my judgment.   *   *   *   We invite

you to go with us in providing, after we shall have
destroyed bribery outside of the polling-booth, that
you shall not have the embodiment of rascality behind
it to vitiate and destroy the purity of elections within.

NATIONAL REPUBLICAN CONVENTION OF 1876.

Mr. Blaine's dash and brilliancy as the Republican
leader on the floor of the House made him the great
popular favorite among the Republican masses, and
brought him prominently forward as a candidate for
the Republican nomination for President in 1876.
Maine, his adopted State, took the lead, the Republican State Convention at Augusta, January 20, 1876,
appointing the first delegation instructed in his favor.
Other Northern States followed, so that he was the
most prominent and the most popular of all the Republican candidates for the nomination. Other prominent
candidates were United States Senators Roscoe Conkling, of New York, and Oliver P. Morton, of Indiana,
and Secretary of the Treasury Benjamin H. Bristow,
of Kentucky. Pennsylvania presented the name of
Governor John F. Hartranft, and Ohio brought forward Governor Rutherford B. Hayes.

In May, 1876, slanderous charges were made in
Congress against Mr. Blaine's character, and the
Democratic Congress instituted an investigation concerning charges concerning his relations with the
Union Pacific Railway ; but Mr. Blaine succeeded in
vindicating himself against these malignant attacks
upon his reputation and strengthened himself in the
affections of the masses. About the time of the meeting of the Republican National Convention at Cincinnati, near the middle of June, 1876, Mr. Blaine fell a victim to sunstroke in Washington, but soon recovered.

The Republican National Convention assembled in Exposition Hall, in Cincinnati, June 14, 1876. Mr. Blaine was the strongest candidate before the Convention, and the organization of the Convention appeared to be in his favor. The first day was occupied with the organization and with speeches from various delegates. The second day of the Convention (June 15, 1876,) was taken up with the adoption of the platform and the naming of candidates. When the roll of States was called, Mr. Kellogg, of Connecticut, nominated Marshall Jewell, of that State; R. W. Thompson, of Indiana, nominated Oliver P. Morton; General Harlan, of Kentucky, nominated Benjamin H. Bristow; Robert G. Ingersoll, of Illinois, nominated James G. Blaine, of Maine, in a neat speech; General Stewart L. Woodford, of New York, nominated Roscoe Conkling; Ex-Governor Noyes, of Ohio, nominated Governor Hayes; and Linn Bartholomew, of Pennsylvania, nominated Governor Hartranft. The following is Col. Ingersoll's speech nominating Mr. Blaine:

"The Republicans of the United States demand as their leader in the great contest of 1876 a man of intelligence, a man of integrity, a man of well-known and approved political opinions. They demand a statesman. They demand a reformer after, as well as before, the election. They demand a politician in the highest, broadest and best sense—a man of superb moral courage. They demand a man acquainted with public affairs, with the wants of the people, with not only the requirements of the hour, but with the demands of the future. They demand a man broad enough to comprehend the relations of this Government to the other nations of the earth. They demand

a man well versed in the powers, duties and prerogatives of each and every department of this Government.
They demand a man who will sacredly preserve the
financial honor of the United States; one who knows
enough to know that the national debt must be paid
through the prosperity of his people; one who knows
enough to know that all the financial theories in the
world cannot redeem a single dollar; one who knows
enough to know that all the money must be made,
not by law, but by labor; one who knows enough to
know that the people of the United States have the
industry to make the money and the honor to pay it
over just as fast as they make it.

The Republicans of the United States demand a man
who knows that prosperity and resumption, when they
come, must come together; that when they come they
will come hand in hand through the golden harvest
fields; hand in hand by the whirling spindles and the
turning wheels; hand in hand past the open furnace
doors; hand in hand by the flaming forges; hand in
hand by the chimneys filled with eager fire, greeted
and grasped by the countless sons of toil.

This money has to be dug out of the earth. You
cannot make it by passing resolutions in a political
convention.

The Republicans of the United States want a man
who knows that this Government should protect every
citizen at home and abroad; who knows that any Government that will not defend its defenders, and protect
its protectors, is a disgrace to the map of the world.
They demand a man who believes in the eternal sep-
aration and divorcement of church and school. They
demand a man whose political reputation is spotless
as a star; but they do not demand that their candidate

shall have a certificate of moral character signed by a Confederate Congress. The man who has, in full, heaped, and rounded measure, all these splendid qualifications, is the present grand and gallant leader of the Republican party—JAMES G. BLAINE.

Our country, crowned with the vast and marvelous achievements of its first century, asks for a man worthy of the past and prophetic of her future; asks for a man who has the audacity of genius ; asks for a man who has the grandest combination of heart, conscience, and brain beneath her flag—such a man is JAMES G. BLAINE.

For the Republican host, led by this intrepid man, there can be no defeat.

This is a grand year—a year filled with the recollections of the Revolution; filled with proud and tender memories of the past—with the sacred legends of Liberty—a year in which the sons of Freedom will drink from the fountains of enthusiasm—a year in which the people call for a man who has preserved in Congress what our soldiers won upon the field—a year in which they call for the man who has torn from the throat of treason the tongue of slander; for the man who has snatched the mask of Democracy from the hideous face of Rebellion ; for the man who, like an intellectual athlete, has stood in the arena of debate and challenged all comers, and who is still a total stranger to defeat.

Like an armed warrior, like a plumed knight, JAMES G. BLAINE marched down the halls of the American Congress and threw his shining lance full and fair against the brazen foreheads of the defamers of his country and the maligners of his honor.   For the Republican party to desert this gallant leader now is as though an army should desert their general upon the field of battle.

JAMES G. BLAINE is now and has been for years the bearer of the sacred standard of the Republican party. I call it sacred, because no human being can stand beneath its folds without becoming and without remaining free.

Gentlemen of the Convention: In the name of the great Republic, the only Republic that ever existed upon this earth ; in the name of all her defenders and of all her supporters ; in the name of all her soldiers living ; in the name of all her soldiers dead upon the field of battle, and in the name of those who perished in the skeleton clutch of famine at Andersonville and Libby, whose sufferings he so vividly remembers, Illinois—Illinois nominates for the next President of this country that prince of parliamentarians, that leader of leaders, JAMES G. BLAINE.

On the third and last day of the convention the balloting for candidates took place with the following results :

CANDIDATES.	First Ballot	Second Ballot	Third Ballot	Fourth Ballot	Fifth Ballot	Sixth Ballot	Seventh Ballot
Blaine	298	296	293	292	286	308	351
Bristow	114	113	121	126	114	111	21
Conkling	93	99	90	84	82	81	
Morton	111	124	113	108	95	85	
Hartranft	63	58	68	71	69	50	
Hayes	64	61	67	68	104	113	384
Jewell	11	11					
Wheeler	3	3	2	2	2	2	
Washburne	1	1	1	3	3	4	

Governor Rutherford Burchard Hayes, of Ohio, having the majority of the whole number of votes, was declared the nominee of the Republican party for President of the United States in 1876. The Hon. Wm. A. Wheeler, of New York, was then nominated for Vice President, and the Convention adjourned *sine die.* Mr. Blaine's failure to receive the nomination was a sad disappointment to the great mass of Republicans throughout the country. To thousands in his native State, Pennsylvania, his defeat came as something like a personal grief. During the campaign Mr. Blaine devoted himself earnestly to the election of Governor Hayes.

IN THE UNITED STATES SENATE.

On July 3d, 1876, Governor Connor, of Maine, appointed James G. Blaine, United States Senator to succeed the Hon. Lot M. Morrill, who had just resigned to accept the post of Secretary of the Treasury, in place of Mr. Bristow, who had just retired from that post. At the next session of the Maine Legislature, Mr. Blaine was elected to his seat in the United States Senate.

The Presidential election of 1876 being disputed, and the country being threatened in consequence with civil war, Congress upon its meeting in December agreed upon a plan to settle the dispute. The plan proposed was adopted by a committee of both houses in the shape of a bill providing for an Electoral Commission to consist of five Senators, five Representatives, and five Supreme Court Judges. The bill was reported, warmly discussed in both Houses, and passed in January, 1877, and the Commission decided in favor of Hayes and Wheeler, the Republican candidates.   Mr. Blaine spoke against the bill, as follows:

MR. PRESIDENT: I have, I trust, as profound an
appreciation as any Senator on this floor of the gravity
of the situation.   I would not, if I could, underrate it,
and no public good can result from overstating it.   I
have felt anxious from the first day of the session to
join in any wise measure that would tend to allay
public uneasiness and to restore, or at least maintain,
public confidence.   In this spirit I followed the lead
of the honorable chairman of the Judiciary Committee (Mr. Edmunds), in December, in an effort to secure
a Constitutional Amendment, which would empower
the Supreme Court of the United States to peacefully
and promptly settle all the troubles growing out of
the disputed Electoral votes.   I knew there were
weighty objections to any measure connecting the
Judiciary with the political affairs of the country;
but I nevertheless thought, and I still think that,
under the impressive sanction of a Constitutional
Amendment, the angry difficulties growing out of a
Presidential contest might with safety and satisfaction
be adjusted by that supreme tribunal which, combining dignity, honor, learning and presumed impartiality, would be regarded by men of all parties as a
trustworthy repository.

It was in that spirit and with these views that I
voted for the Constitutional Amendment, which I regret to say failed to commend itself to the Senate.   It
was defeated, and I refer to it now only to show that
I have not been reluctant to make any proper and
Constitutional adjustment of pending difficulties.   I
am not wedded to any particular plan except that of
the Constitution, nor have I any pet theories outside
of the Constitution, and, unlike a good many gentle-

men on both sides of the chamber with whom I am newly associated here, I have no embarrassing record on this question of " counting the votes."

But. Mr. President, looking at the measure under consideration and looking at it with every desire to co-operate with those who are so warmly advocating it, I am compelled to withhold the support of my vote. I am not prepared to vest any body of men with the tremendous power which this bill gives to fourteen gentlemen, four of whom are to complete their number by selecting a fifteenth. and selecting a fifteenth under such circumstances as throughout the length and breadth of the land impart a peculiar interest, I might say an absorbing interest to what Mr. Benton termed in the Texas indemnity bill, " that coy and bashful blank." I do not believe that Congress itself has the power which it proposes to confer on these fifteen gentlemen. I do not profess to be what is termed, in the current phrase of the day, a " Constitutional lawyer," but every Senator voting under the obligations of his oath and his conscience must ultimately be his own Constitutional lawyer. And I deliberately say that I do not believe that Congress possesses the power itself, and still less the power to transfer to any body of fourteen, or fifteen, or fifty gentlemen, that with which it is now proposed to invest five Senators, five Representatives and five Judges of the Supreme Court. I did not at this late hour of the night rise to make an argument, but merely to state the ground, the Constitutional and conscientious ground, on which I feel compelled to vote against the pending bill. I have had a great desire to co-operate with my political friends who are advocating it, but every possible inclination of that kind has been re-

moved and dispelled by the very arguments brought
in support of the bill, able and exhaustive as they
have been on that side of the question.

I beg to make one additional remark through you,
Mr. President, to the Chairman of the Judiciary Committee, that while this subject is now in the public
mind as it never has been before from the foundation
of the Government, when the leading jurists of the
country have been investigating it as never before,
that they will not allow this session of Congress to
close without carefully maturing and submitting to the
States a Constitutional Amendment which will remove
so far as possible all embarrassment in the future.
The people of this country, without regard to party,
desire in our Government due and orderly procedure
under the sanction of law, and that I am sure is what
is desired by every Senator on this floor and by none
more ardently than by myself.   Let us then, if possible, guard against all trouble in the future by some
wise and timely measure that will be just to all parties
and all sections, and, above all, just to our obligations
under the Constitution.

Senator Blaine opposed President Hayes' Southern
policy, and took a decided stand against the President's
action in recognizing the Democratic State Governments in South Carolina and Louisiana in the Spring
of 1877.

When the Senate considered the bill authorizing
the free coinage of the standard silver dollar and to
restore its legal-tender character, Mr. Blaine offered
a substitute for the bill, containing three propositions,
as he states in these words:

1. That the dollar shall contain four hundred and

twenty-five grains of standard silver, shall have un-limited coinage, and be an unlimited legal tender.

2. That all profits of coinage shall go to the Government, and not to the operator in silver bullion.

3. That silver dollars or silver bullion, assayed and mint-stamped, may be deposited with the Assistant Treasurer of New York, for which coin-certificates may be issued, the same in denomination as United States notes, not below ten dollars, and that these shall be redeemable on demand in coin or bullion, thus furnishing a paper circulation based on an actual deposit of precious metal, giving us notes as valuable as those of the Bank of England, and doing away at once with the dreaded inconvenience of silver on account of bulk and weight.

Mr. Blaine presented his views on the Silver Question, in a rather lengthy and very able speech, on the day he offered his substitute, which was February 7, 1878.

The concluding portion of his speech reads thus:

The effect of paying the labor of this country in silver coin of full value, as compared with the irredeemable paper, or as compared even with silver of inferior value, will make itself felt in a single generation to the extent of tens of millions, perhaps hundreds of millions, in the aggregate savings which represent consolidated capital. It is the instinct of man from the savage to the scholar—developed in childhood and remaining with age—to value the metals which in all tongues are called precious. Excessive paper money leads to extravagance, to waste, and to want, as we painfully witness on all sides to-day. And in

6

the midst of the proof of its demoralizing and de-
structive effect, we hear it proclaimed in the Halls of
Congress that " the people demand cheap money." I
deny it. I declare such a phrase to be a total mis-
apprehension—a total misinterpretation of the popular wish. The people do not demand cheap money.
They demand an abundance of good money, which is
an entirely different thing. They do not want a single
gold standard, that will exclude silver and benefit
those already rich. They do not want an inferior
silver standard, that will drive out gold and not help
those already poor. They want both metals, in full
value, in equal honor, in whatever abundance the
bountiful earth will yield them to the searching eye
of science and to the hard hand of labor.

The two metals have existed, side by side, in har-
monious, honorable companionship as money, ever
since intelligent trade was known among men. It is
well nigh forty centuries since " Abraham weighed
to Ephron four hundred shekels of silver—current
money with the merchant." Since that time nations
have risen and fallen, races have disappeared, dialects
and languages have been forgotten, arts have been
lost, treasures have perished, continents have been
discovered, islands have been sunk in the sea, and
through all these ages and through all these changes
silver and gold have reigned supreme, as the representatives of value, as the media of exchange. The
dethronement of each has been attempted in turn,
and sometimes the dethronement of both; but always
in vain! And we are here to-day, deliberating anew
over the problem which comes down to us from Abraham's time—*the weight of the silver*, that shall be
" current money with the merchant."

[As Mr. Blaine resumed his seat there was protracted applause in portions of the galleries.]

The following is an extract from Senator Blaine's Speech on the Currency, at Biddeford, Maine, delivered August 21st, 1878:

By common consent the currency question is the great question before the people. This I regret; because, if there is one thing people cannot afford, it is a political currency question. Let us settle it, and settle it right. Let us review the circumstances that brought us where we are now. In 1861 an extra session of Congress was called, and it authorized the Treasurer to borrow $400,000,000, as there was no money in the Treasury. Fifty millions of demand notes were also authorized, and when Congress assembled after the Christmas holidays they assembled with an empty Treasury. In this particular strait the Government provided for an issuance of $150,-000,000 of legal-tender notes. That was a measure of absolute necessity. It was useless to stand upon a very fine drawn point at such a time. It was a question of life. We declared the notes legal tender. Before another year had expired we were called upon to issue another $150,000,000, and when Congress assembled in December, 1863, the report of the Secretary of the Treasury brought before us a very embarrassing condition. The Government was without currency again. We were at that time appealing to every civilized nation of the world for money. Forty or fifty million dollars were due the army, and ready cash was demanded. Out of this state of affairs came the Loan Act, which really supplied funds which were necessary for the salvation of the

Nation. The Loan Act had not only authority of law, but in a peculiar and strong sense it is binding upon us. In this act was a proviso as follows: " That the total amount of those notes issued, and to be issued, shall never exceed $400,000,000." It was the price which in extreme urgency we pledged ourselves to, and if there is any honor in the American people they would as soon sign away their birthright as violate this pledge. The *most fearful thing that could happen to this country would be the issuance of an unlimited amount of currency. How are you going to contract the currency? You want Republican money or Democratic money, do you not?

Whatever else the American people do with currency, let me say to you that there is no body of men so little competent to determine the question of money as Congressmen. I voted in Congress for the Greenback bill. I voted that greenbacks should not be contracted.

Greenback people say that we should not have any banks. For seven hundred years we have had banks, and we could not conduct the business of the country for a minute without banks. Why are banks a necessity? A bank is a place where the borrower of money meets the lender; where surplus money is deposited Suppose a man wants to borrow $10,000 to go into business. Greenbackers would send him all over the country borrowing $50 here and $50 there. There are at the present time three bills in Congress for "resurrecting" the State Banks. New-England enjoyed, under the old system, the best banks in the country, but they owed their reputation to the personal integrity of the men who stood behind the counter. The speaker aptly illustrated the weakness of the system by referring to the Lumberman's Bank, which might be said to have been owned by the present Greenback candidate for Governor. This bank had a capital of $50,000, but at one time had on hand unsigned bills to the amount of $165,000, which would be signed as fast as anybody wanted them. In fact, the old system of banking was based upon the personal notes of the stockholders. If you will have banks, then what kind will you have: responsible or irresponsible? National banks are perfectly free for every man to engage in with just one little condition that the Government insists upon—that you shall not issue any bills until you have put into the United States Treasury an account equal to ten per cent. additional to protect the bill-holders.

If you hold a National bank bill, you don't care whether the bank is burst or not. In regard to taxing bonds, Greenbackers say "here is an exempted class." The only man in the United States who pays absolutely full tax on his property is the holder of Government bonds; for instance: A invests $10,000 in Government 4 per cents; B invests an equal amount in Maine State 6s, and C invests a like amount in Maine Central 7 per cents. In the first case the investor in Government bonds pays his taxes in advance, but in the case of the other bonds, is it within your experience that holders thereof flock to the assessor's office asking to be taxed? Facts show that but a very small portion of the bonds are taxed. It is the easiest thing in the world for your brother in California to own them, or your uncle in some other part of the country. Then why delude yourselves with the idea that if you tax Government bonds they would be any more likely to turn up for taxation

than these State or railroad bonds? If you succeed
in taxing bonds you merely place upon your shoulders
an additional burden of $40,000,000. Government
bonds never could nor never should be taxed. There
are five kinds of money that the United States stands
sponsor for: gold and silver—and gold is better than
silver. Moses, in the second chapter of Genesis, tells
us "that gold is good;" and it makes no difference
whether it is stamped by the United States or Vene-
zuela. Then there is the old-fashioned, war-honored
patriotic greenback, that did such great work, that
says the United States will pay $10, or as it may be,
reserving to the United States when they would pay.
In 1875 it did say when they would pay, viz.: January 1, 1879. The advance school of Greenbackers,
represented by General Butler, don't want this kind
of greenback at all. They want another kind. They
don't want anything stamped with "promise to pay."
They want this greenback to say, "this is $10," or
any sum. Such talk is merely nonsense. Why not
say, "this is horse," why not make it $1,000? It takes
no more paper or time to print it, but it is not so with
gold. The next government money is National Bank
bills, and lastly the silver certificates.

We fancied during the Greenback craze that we
were all getting rich. In 1873 we found out we had
been buying $800,000,000 more than we were selling.
There is nothing so mysterious about National finances. The same principles are involved in private
finances. If a farmer is buying more than he is selling from his farm, he is growing poorer, but if he is
selling more than he is buying, he is getting richer.
This idea holds good with the trade of the country.
Now things are changed. We are buying less abroad

and have a balance in our favor of $630,000,000. No people in the world are so able to maintain a specie basis as the United States, if they say they will. We are just in sight of the day of redemption. We can look right into the promised land, but Greenbackers say, " Don't go in. Come, now, and wander with us for years more." You depreciate your currency, and you might as well by one shock of mighty power paralyze capital from one end of the country to the other. You reduce the country from that of a great commercial people to a beggarly small retail affair. The things which this day frighten men are wild schemes of finance. What the United States needs in this matter is a large amount of " let-alone-ativeness." You cannot keep this currency as a political foot-ball. You cannot settle this question until you settle it right.

The following is Senator Blaine's speech in the U. S. Senate, December 11, 1878 :

MR. PRESIDENT: The pending resolution was offered by me with a two-fold purpose in view. First, to place on record in a definited and authentic form, the frauds and outrages by which some recent elections were carried by the Democratic Party in the Southern States ; second, to find if there be any method by which a repetition of these crimes against a free ballot may be prevented.

The newspaper is the channel through which the people of the United States are informed of current events, and the accounts given in the press represent the elections in some of the Southern States to have been accompanied by violence, in not a few cases reaching the destruction of life ; to have been controlled by threats that awed and intimidated a large

class of voters; to have been manipulated by fraud
of the most shameless and shameful description. Indeed, in South Carolina there seems to have been no
election at all in any proper sense of the term. There
was, instead, a series of skirmishes over the State, in
which the polling-places were regarded as forts to be
captured by one party and held against the other,
and where this could not be done with convenience,
frauds in the count and tissue-ballot devices were resorted to in order to effectually destroy the voice of
the majority. These, in brief, are the accounts given
in the non-partisan press of the disgraceful outrages
that attended the recent elections, and so far as I
have seen, these statements are without serious con-
tradiction. It is but just and fair to all parties, however, that an impartial investigation of the facts
shall be made by a committee of the Senate, proceeding under the authority of law, and representing the
power of the nation. Hence my resolution.

But we do not need investigation to establish certain facts already of official record. We know that
one hundred and six Representatives in Congress
were recently chosen in the States formerly slave-
holding, and that the Democrats elected one hundred
and one, or possibly one hundred and two, and the
Republicans four, or possibly five. We know that
thirty-five of these Representatives were assigned to
the Southern States by reason of the colored population, and that the entire political power thus founded
on the numbers of the colored people has been seized
and appropriated to the aggrandizement of its own
strength by the Democratic party of the South.

The issue thus raised before the country, Mr. President, is not one of mere sentiment for the rights of

the negro—though far distant be the day when the rights of any American citizen, however black or however poor, shall form the mere dust of the balance in any controversy; nor is the issue one that involves the waving of the "bloody shirt," to quote the elegant vernacular of Democratic vituperation; nor still further is the issue as now presented only a question of the equality of the black voter of the South with the white voter of the South; the issue. Mr. President, has taken a far wider range, one of portentous magnitude, and that is, whether the white voter of the North shall be equal to the white voter of the South in shaping the policy and fixing the destiny of this country; or whether, to put it still more baldly, the white man who fought in the ranks of the Union Army shall have as weighty and influential a vote in the Government of the Republic as the white man who fought in the ranks of the rebel army. The one fought to uphold, the other to destroy, the Union of the States, and to-day he who fought to destroy is a far more important factor in the government of the nation than he who fought to uphold it.

Let me illustrate my meaning by comparing groups of States of the same representative strength North and South. Take the States of South Carolina, Mississippi and Louisiana. They send seventeen Representatives to Congress. Their aggregate population is composed of 1,035,000 whites, and 1,224,000 colored; the colored being nearly 200,000 in excess of the whites. Of the seventeen Representatives, then, it is evident that nine were apportioned to these States by reason of their colored population, and only eight by reason of their white population; and yet,

in the choice of the entire seventeen Representatives,
the colored voters had no more voice or power than
their remote kindred on the shores of Senegambia or
on the Gold Coast.   The 1,035,000 white people had
the sole and absolute choice of the entire seventeen
Representatives.   In contrast, take two States in the
North, Iowa and Wisconsin, with seventeen Representatives.   They have a white population of 2,247,-
000—considerably more than double the entire white
population of the three Southern States I have named.
In Iowa and Wisconsin, therefore, it takes 132,000
white population to send a Representative to Congress, but in South Carolina, Mississippi, and Louisiana every 60,000 white people send a Representative.
In other words, 60,000 white people in those Southern
States have precisely the same political power in the
government of the country that 132,000 white people
have in Iowa and Wisconsin.

Take another group of seventeen Representatives
from the South and from the North.   Georgia and
Alabama have a white population of 1,158,000 and a
colored population of 1,020,000.   They send seventeen
Representatives to Congress, of whom nine were apportioned on account of the white population, and
eight on account of the colored population.   But the
colored voters are not able to choose a single Representative, the white Democrats choosing the whole
seventeen.   The four Northern States, Michigan,
Minnesota, Nebraska and California, have seventeen
Representatives, based on a white population of 2,250,-
000, or almost double the white population of Georgia
and Alabama, so that in these relative groups of States
we find the white man South exercises by his vote
double the political power of the white man North.

Let us carry the comparison to a more comprehensive generalization. The eleven States that formed the Confederate Government had by the last census a population of 9,500,000, of which in round numbers 5,500,000 were white and 4,000,000 colored. On this aggregate population seventy-three Representatives in Congress were apportioned to those States—forty-two or forty-three of which were by reason of the white population, and thirty or thirty-one by reason of the colored population. At the recent election the white Democracy of the South seized seventy of the seventy-three districts, and thus secured a Democratic majority in the next House of Representatives. Thus it appears that throughout the States that formed the late Confederate Government 75,000 whites—the very people that rebelled against the Union—are enabled to elect a Representative in Congress, while in the loyal States it requires 132,000 of the white people that fought for the Union to elect a Representative. In levying every tax, therefore, in making every appropriation of money, in fixing every line of public policy, in decreeing what shall be the fate and fortune of the Republic, the Confederate soldier South is enabled to cast a vote that is twice as powerful and twice as influential as the vote of the Union soldier North.

But the white men of the South did not acquire, and do not hold this superior power by reason of law or justice, but in disregard and defiance of both. The Fourteenth Amendment of the Constitution was expected to be, and was designed to be, a preventive and corrective of all such possible abuses. The reading of the clause applicable to the case is instructive and suggestive. Hear it:

Representatives shall be apportioned among the
several States according to their respective numbers,
counting the whole number of persons in each State,
excluding Indians not taxed. But when the right to
vote at any election for the choice of Electors for
President and Vice-President of the United States,
Representatives in Congress, the executive and judicial officers of a State, or the members of the Legislature thereof, is denied to any of the male inhabitants of such State, being twenty-one years of age,
and citizens of the United States, or in any way
abridged, except for participation in rebellion, or
other crime, the basis of representation therein shall
be reduced in the proportion which the number of
such male citizens shall bear to the whole number of
male citizens twenty-one years of age in such State.

The patent, undeniable intent of this provision was
that if any class of voters were denied or in any way
abridged in their right of suffrage, then the class so
denied or abridged should not be counted in the basis
of representation ; or, in other words, that no State
or States should gain a large increase of representation in Congress by reason of counting any class of
population not permitted to take part in electing such
Representatives.   But the construction given to this
provision is that before any forfeiture of representation
can be enforced, the denial or abridgment of suffrage
must be the result of a law specifically enacted by the
State.   Under this construction every negro voter
may have his suffrage absolutely denied or fatally
abridged by the violence, actual or threatened, of irre-
sponsible mobs, or by frauds and deceptions of State
officers, from the Governor down to the last election
clerk ; and then, unless some State law can be shown
that authorizes the denial or abridgment, the State
escapes all penalty or peril of reduced representation.

This construction may be upheld by the courts ruling on the letter of the law, " which killeth," but the spirit of justice cries aloud against the evasive and atrocious conclusion that deals out oppression to the innocent and shields the guilty from the legitimate consequences of willful transgression.

The colored citizen is thus most unhappily situated ; his right of suffrage is but a hollow mockery ; it holds to his ear the word of promise but breaks it always to his hope, and he ends only in being made the unwilling instrument of increasing the political strength of that party from which he received ever-tightening fetters when he was a slave and contemptuous refusal of civil rights since he was made free. He resembles, indeed, those unhappy captives in the East, who, deprived of their birthright, are compelled to yield their strength to the upbuilding of the monarch from whose tyrannies they have most to fear, and to fight against the power from which alone deliverance might be expected. The franchise intended for the shield and defense of the negro has been turned against him and against his friends, and has vastly increased the power of those from whom he has nothing to hope and everything to dread.

The political power thus appropriated by Southern Democrats by reason of the negro population amounts to thirty-five Representatives in Congress. It is massed almost solidly, and offsets the great State of New York; or Pennsylvania and New Jersey together; or the whole of New England; or Ohio and Indiana united; or the combined strength of Illinois, Minnesota, Kansas, California, Nevada, Nebraska, Colorado and Oregon. The seizure of this power is wanton usurpation; it is flagrant outrage; it is vio-

lent perversion of the whole theory of republican
government. It inures solely to the present advantage, and yet, I believe, to the permanent dishonor of
the Democratic party. It is by reason of this tramp-
ling down of human rights, this ruthless seizure of
unlawful power, that the Democratic party holds the
popular branch of Congress to-day, and will in less
than ninety days have control of this body also, thus
grasping the entire legislative department of the Government through the unlawful capture of the Southern
States. If the proscribed vote of the South were
cast as its lawful owners desire, the Democratic party
could not gain power. Nay, if it were not counted
on the other side against the instincts and the interests, against the principles and prejudices of its lawful owners, Democratic success would be hopeless.
It is not enough, then, for modern Democratic tactics
that the negro vote shall be silenced; the demand
goes further, and insists that it shall be counted on
their side, that all the Representatives in Congress
and all the Presidential Electors apportioned by reason of the negro vote shall be so cast and so governed as to insure Democratic success—regardless of
justice, in defiance of law.

    And this injustice is wholly unprovoked. I doubt
if it be in the power of the most searching investigation to show, that in any Southern State, during the
period of Republican control, any legal voter was
ever debarred from the freest exercise of his suffrage.
Even the revenges, which would have leaped into life
with many who despised the negro, were buried out of
sight with a magnanimity which the "superior race"
fail to follow and seem reluctant to recognize. I
know it is said in retort of such charges against the

Southern elections, as I am now reviewing, that un-
fairness of equal gravity prevails in Northern elections.   I hear it in many quarters and read it in the
papers that in the late exciting election in Massachusetts intimidation and bull-dozing, if not so rough and
rancorous as in the South, were yet as wide-spread
and effective.

I have read, and yet I refuse to believe, that the
distinguished gentleman who made an energetic, but
unsuccessful, canvass for the Governorship of that
State, has indorsed and approved these charges, and
I have accordingly made my resolution broad enough
to include their thorough investigation.   I am not
demanding fair elections in the South without demanding fair elections in the North also.   But venturing to
speak for the New England States, of whose laws and
customs I know something, I dare assert that in the
late election in Massachusetts, or any of her neighboring Commonwealths, it will be impossible to find even
one case where a voter was driven from the polls,
where a voter did not have the fullest, fairest, freest
opportunity to cast the ballot of his choice, and have
it honestly and faithfully counted in the returns.
Suffrage on this continent was first made universal in
New England, and in the administration of their affairs
her people have found no other appeal necessary than
that which is addressed to their honesty of conviction and to their intelligent self-interest.   If there be
anything different to disclose, I pray you show it to
us that we may amend our ways.

But whenever a feeble protest is made against such
injustice, as I have described in the South, the re-
ponse we get comes to us in the form of a taunt.
" What are you going to do about it?" and " How do

you propose to help yourselves?" This is the stereotyped answer of defiance which intrenched Wrong
always gives to inquiring Justice; and those who
imagine it to be conclusive do not know the temper
of the American people. For, let me assure you, that
against the complicated outrage upon the right of
representation, lately triumphant in the South, there
will be arrayed many phases of public opinion in the
North not often hitherto in harmony. Men who have
cared little, and affected to care less, for the rights or
the wrongs of the negro, suddenly find that vast mone-
tary and commercial interests, great questions of revenue adjustments of tariff, vast investments in manufactures, in railways, and in mines, are under the
control of a Democratic Congress, whose majority was
obtained by depriving the negro of his rights under
a common Constitution and common laws. Men who
have expressed disgust with the "waving of bloody
shirts," and have been offended with talk about negro
equality, are beginning to perceive that the pending
question of to-day relates more pressingly to the
equality of white men under this Government, and
that however careless they may be about the rights
or the wrongs of the negro, they are very jealous and
tenacious about the rights of their own race, and
the dignity of their own fire-sides and their own
kindred.

I know something of public opinion in the North.
I know a great deal about the views, wishes and purposes of the Republican party of the Nation. Within
that entire great organization there is not one man,
whose opinion is entitled to be quoted, that does not
desire peace and harmony and friendship, and a
patriotic and fraternal union between the North and

the South. This wish is spontaneous, instinctive, universal throughout the Northern States; and yet, among men of character and sense, there is surely no need of attempting to deceive ourselves as to the precise truth. First pure, then peaceable. Gush will not remove a grievance, and no disguise of State rights will close the eyes of our people to the necessity of correcting a great national wrong. Nor should the South make the fatal mistake of concluding that injustice to the negro is not also injustice to the white man; nor should it ever be forgotten that for the wrongs of both a remedy will assuredly be found. The war, with all its costly sacrifices, was fought in vain, unless equal rights for all classes be established in all the States of the Union; and now, in words which are those of friendship, however differently they may be accepted, I tell the men of the South here on this floor and beyond this chamber, that even if they could strip the negro of his Constitutional rights they can never permanently maintain the inequality of white men in this Nation—they can never make a white man's vote in the South doubly as powerful in the administration of the Government as a white man's vote in the North.

In a memorable debate in the House of Commons, Mr. Macaulay reminded Daniel O'Connell, when he was moving for repeal, that the English Whigs had endured calumny, abuse, popular fury, loss of position, exclusion from Parliament, rather than the great Agitator himself should be less than a British subject; and Mr. Macaulay warned him that they would never suffer him to be more. Let me now remind you, that the Government, under whose protecting flag we sit to-day, sacrificed myriads of lives and ex-

7

tended thousands of millions of treasure that our countrymen of the South should remain citizens of the United States, having equal personal rights and equal political privileges with all other citizens. And I venture, now and here, to warn the men of the South, in the exact words of Macaulay, that we will never suffer them to be more!

[Upon the conclusion of Mr. Blaine's speech there was considerable applause in the galleries, but it was soon checked by the Vice-President.]

On the 22d of April, 1878, Mr. Blaine offered the following resolutions:

Resolved, That any radical change in our present Tariff laws would, in the judgment of the Senate, be inopportune, would needlessly derange the business interests of the country, and would seriously retard that return to prosperity for which all should earnestly co-operate.

Resolved, That, in the judgment of the Senate, it should be the fixed policy of this Government, to so maintain our Tariff for revenue as to afford adequate protection to American labor.

On the 1st of May, 1878, Mr. Blaine called up his resolutions and urged their passage. He objected to the appointment of a Tariff Commission, in regard to which he said:

I think one of the most mischievous measures in its effects, not of course so designed by the gentleman who may move it, would be to have a roving Commission on the idea that, when they get through running hither and thither over the country, and examining this way and that way about the tariff, certain recommendations are to be made and certain changes

are to take place. Nothing would more effectually
unsettle the business of the country than that. That
is only having the agitation of the subject, which is
now disturbing the country by its appearance in Congress, transferred to a Commission. You only elon-
gate the evil, you only increase it, you only keep drawing it out over a long time. There is no form, in my
judgment, which the tariff discussion or tariff legislation could take that would be fraught with more
mischief to the country than to have a Commission
sitting upon it. After they had made their report, it
could not effect legislation here or influence the opinion of any person in either branch of Congress one
way or the other. We have had many of these com-
missions upon divers and sundry subjects, and I have
never known them to do a particle of good, so far as
producing a result in practical legislation.

After which Senator Beck of Kentucky launched
out on a tirade against our Tariff laws, in response to
which Mr. Blaine said :

Mr. PRESIDENT: The honorable Senator from Kentucky (Mr. Beck) quite prematurely, and without
my expectation, launched forth into an argument on
the subject of the Tariff; and very naturally, taking
the side he does, he quarrels with the civilization of
the nineteenth century. He says it is the machinery
that is to blame. We have got machinery in this
country, he says, that will do the work of one hundred and seventy-five million men, and there is where
all the trouble is. Of course the logical result of the
Senator's argument is to abolish the locomotive, the
steam engine and all modern appliances of transportation and manufacture, and go back to the hand-
loom and the wagon.

MR. BECK. Oh, no; I beg pardon.

MR. BLAINE. I did not interrupt the Senator, and I hope he will allow me to get through my argument.

MR. BECK. You surely will not say that I intended any such thing as that.

MR. BLAINE. I do not see any other result. The Senator sayst he whole trouble grows out of the fact, that we have labor-saving machinery.

MR. BECK. Allow me to put the Senator right there. My argument was that we need no protection because we have machinery equal to any other machinery, and that machinery can compete in the markets of the world. I wish we had more.

MR. BLAINE. The Senator said—he may correct his argument now—that we had the machinery here, which was the slave of the owners of it, that they could command it to stand still or to turn when they chose. that the laborer was their servant, and that he had no independence outside of the machinery. I do not understand any logical result, or see how the Senator can free the laborer from the position he puts him in. but by abolishing the machinery, I do not understand it otherwise. And I think among the anomalies that American politics turn up—and we meet many of them in this Chamber—among the strange contradictions that history develops, is that the seat of Henry Clay, in the Senate of the United States, should be the place from which a free-trade argument to overthrow the American System and take the side of the Free-Trader should be made. It is one of the anomalies of American politics; and the argument of the Senator from Kentucky goes right back to what was said before the war by a distinguished Southern man, that he hoped to see the day when the old barter between the English ship that was anchored in the Savannah or the Potomac, or the Cooper or the Ashley, should be resumed with the planter who shipped directly to England; and it is that spirit to-day which holds in manacles and paralyzes the development of the Southern country.

The Senator recalled to us the great Tariff of Rob't J. Walker, and cited to us the vast achievement of political philosophy and economy that man presented to us in his three reports of 1845, 1846, and 1847. Well, the Tariff of Robert J. Walker had abundant opportunity to " run and be glorified" in this country, and it ran us into bankruptcy and want and ruin. It was modified in 1857, going still further in the same direction. The years 1857, 1858, 1859, and 1860 were years of prostration and financial ruin, and wide-spread disaster and want, in which the laborer was not employed. Those four years were much more severe in many portions of this country than even the four past years which we have just gone through.

So, when the Senator presents to us the fact that Robert J. Walker established the Tariff of 1846, he presents it as a beacon of warning to every man who remembers its effect throughout the length and breadth of the manufacturing industries of this country.

There we see developed a little collison between our friends on the other side. When the Senator from Kentucky (Mr. Beck) was laying down the Simon Pure Democratic doctrine as it was announced at the last National sanhedrim of that party, the Senator from Pennsylvania (Mr. Wallace) put in an exception, and the Senator from Pennsylvania said that it

was fully understood that the Free-Trade side of the
Tariff question was not to be a Democratic doctrine,
but that all the Congressional districts were to be
left to determine that matter for themselves. Everybody knows that was a contrivance got up for the
benefit of gentlemen placed exactly in the delicate
attitude of the Senator from Pennsylvania, who have
Protective-Tariff constituents behind, allied with the
Free-Trade party in the country at large, and the guise
which was made and attempted for the benefit of Mr.
Greeley in his campaign, was boldly thrown off at St.
Louis when Mr. Tilden became the standard-bearer.

The Senator from Kentucky warned us that the
trouble is radical, and he called up the fact of an
American ship being launched a few days since on
the Delaware; and he said you may build that ship at
the same rate that an English ship is, load her with
goods manufactured in this country as cheaply as in
England, and send her to her port, and the trouble is
she has nothing to bring back. I wish the Senator
would give me his attention this moment.

Mr. Beck. I am trying to.

Mr. Blaine. The trouble is that we have nothing
to bring back, the Senator says. Well, he was sing-
ularly unfortunate in his allusion, because of a total
export annually from Brazil of less than $90,000,000,
we take $40,000,000; of a total export from Brazil of
$500,000,000 within the last six years we have taken
well-nigh $250,000,000. The Senator says the trouble
is that we may sail our ships wherever we please, but
we can get no return cargo. I suppose the idea is
that we had better take our coffee and dyewoods and
other things of that sort from Brazil in British bot-
toms.

MR. BECK. Will the Senator allow me to say, that I referred to vessels sailing to Valparaiso and trading with Chili? and every fact I stated is true, and I hold evidence in my hand, compiled by Mr. Wells in a little work that the Senator from Maine would do well to read, giving exactly the facts that I stated. As to Brazil, we have more trade with her because coffee has been made free lately; and that is the only reason we trade with Brazil.

MR. BLAINE. We took scarcely less coffee when it was taxed.

MR. BECK. I never mentioned Brazil in my remarks.

MR. BLAINE. The Senator mentioned the City of Para and the port to which she was destined to run. The City of Para was launched for a Brazilian line, and all the parade of Congress and the President that went over there was to inaugurate that line. Is not that the fact? You may mention any other South American port, but you do not change the argument a particle. We take a great deal more from all these countries than we send to them, and yet the Senator says the trouble is we can get no return cargo. His argument does not stand at all. Mr. President, there is no more hurtful agitation to-day in this country than the agitation of the Tariff. The Senator talks of a lobby being here. That is always the cry, when anything comes up "there is a lobby!" Has the Senator seen a Tariff lobby here?

MR. BECK. I served upon the Committee of Ways and Means in the House under the distinguished Senator from Massachusetts (Mr. Dawes), and our room was full of them, from the time we met until we adjourned, demanding more protection.

Mr. Blaine. When the gentleman was on the Committee of Ways and Means the persons interested in the Tariff were coming there to give testimony; they were coming to give just what you propose now to get a Commission to give. They were coming in there to give you voluntarily what you propose to get a roving Commission rambling all over the country to inquire into.

Mr. Beck. I am not a member of the present Committee on Finance, and how far their rooms are filled I cannot tell, but I know that there are men here from all parts of the country resisting the reduction of the Tariff.

Mr. Blaine. Very well. Now I ask the Senator from Kentucky another question. Does he know of, has he seen a petition presented in either House of Congress at the present session for a repeal or modification of the present Tariff?

Mr. Beck. I will answer the Senator that the great unorganized mass of the people have nobody to speak for them.

Mr. Blaine. Ah!

Mr. Beck. It is only the classes that are interested who come here. Did the Senator ever know of petitions asking for a reduction of taxes?

Mr. Blaine. What is to hinder the great unorganized mass of people out in Kentucky sending petitions to their distinguished Senators to be presented here?

Mr. Beck. Because they have to rely on their Representatives on this floor and the other to speak for them; but it is men who want something, special protection, to tax all the people to give them more, that are always here asking for more. Of course the people who are interested are scattered all over the country, and can neither organize nor get together. They have no clubs, they have no rings, they have no associations through which they can speak.

MR. DAWES. The Senator from Kentucky has alluded to his service upon the Committee of Ways and Means in the House of Representatives, and said that the room of the Committee of Ways and Means was crowded with men demanding more protection. Does the Senator mean to say that there was one more man in the room of the Committee of Ways and Means demanding protection than there were men demanding that the Tariff should be reduced? Does not the Senator know that there were organizations represented before the committee, whose sole purpose it was to institute just such a tariff as the Tariff of 1846? They had their organs here; they had their office in this city; they had their bureau; they had their men employed on a salary here who were in the room of the Committee of Ways and Means, day in and day out, urging their consideration upon the Committee; and the result of it all was that they were discomfited and routed in the argument, and they have been quiet from that day to this.

MR. BECK. I never heard of organizations of that sort. There may have been, and the Senator from Massachusetts may know of them.

MR. DAWES. If the Senator from Kentucky has forgotten the names of those who represented those organizations, I can give them to him.

MR. BECK. What organizations were they?

MR. DAWES. There was an organization represented by a man by the name of Grosvenor, from Missouri here, who had a bureau on Pennsylvania avenue, and

who urged upon that Committee a system of tariff
which would put the manufactured article below the
raw material in the duty; and when I suggested to
him to make a tariff, and bring it to the committee-
room, which would raise a revenue that would defray
the expenses of the Government and pay the interest
on the national debt upon his principle, and I would
submit it,he utterly failed and confessed his inability
to do it. The Committee of Ways and Means had to
meet this question to raise revenue for the country and
pay the interest on the public debt, and say whether
they would put the duty for that purpose on the raw
material or upon the manufactured article, and the
Committee of Ways and Means came to the conclusion, after having heard all parties, that it was wiser to
put it upon the manufactured article than upon the
raw material; and the policy of that Committee was
to put the raw material, wherever it was produced, at
the door of the shop of the manufacturer as cheaply
as it was possible to do it, taking off the duty and
reducing the transportation, putting it at the door of
the manufacturer as cheaply as possible, and put the
duty upon tea and coffee and upon the manufactured
articles to meet the exigencies of the country.

MR. BLAINE. But there was one very remarkable
exception of raw material, and that was hemp, which
was produced by the State of Kentucky. While they
took good care to make almost all other raw materials cheap, I think the honorable Senator from Kentucky wisely looked out for his own State, and got a
very large duty put on hemp, jute, and all kindred
grasses.

MR. BECK. I desire to say to the Senator from
Maine and the Senator from Massachusetts, that they

are unfortunate in their facts, because they are not true. That is a sufficient answer to them, and the record will show it; and I will show it here when I get an opportunity.

MR. BLAINE. All I know on that point is that the Senator from Kentucky was a member of the Committee of Ways and Means, and that in the tariff bill reported there was a very large protection, which I believe still exists, on hemp. It was exceptionally large, as contrasted with the other raw materials needed for the manufactures of this country, and I always gave credit to the Senator from Kentucky, who is a watchful and able and zealous representative of his constituents, for getting that protection put in. He took good care to have his own door-step swept very clean, but seems to have cared very little about what became of his neighbors.

MR. BECK. That is all very smart. I have answered that the facts are not so, and I will show it to-morrow when I get a chance.

MR. BLAINE. If the Senator can show that there has not been, from the time he was a member of the Committee of Ways and Means, an exceptionally heavy duty on hemp, then he can show that I am mistaken, and I will very gracefully, or as gracefully as I can, acknowledge it; but I think the Senator from Kentucky will not be quite able to show the fact. I do not wish to trench upon the time given to other measures before the Senate; but this matter I hope will come up when we can have a freer discussion.

Here the debate closed.

On the Bill making appropriations for Arrears of Pensions, March 1, 1878, Senator Blaine spoke as follows:

Mr. President.   The Senator from Ohio (Mr. Thurman) indulged himself in a line of remark which I
hardly think was justifiable.   He was arraigning this
entire side of the Chamber for running at the name
of Jefferson Davis.   I wish to say to the honorable
Senator from Ohio, and to all the Senators on that
side, that, neither in this Chamber nor in the other
in which I have served, did I ever hear what he would
call an attack made on Jefferson Davis, until he was
borne into the Chamber for some favor to be asked
and some vote to be exacted.   Who brought him here
to-night?   Who has brought him into Congress at
different times?   No Republican.   No Republican Senator or Representative has ever asked censure or com-
ment, or reference to him; but you bring him here
and ask us either to vote or keep silent; and if we
don't keep silent, then the honorable Senator is as-
tonished and indignant, and the honorable Senator
from Mississippi (Mr. Lamar) thinks that a wanton
insult is intended.   I want the country to understand
that it is that side of the Chamber and not this side
that brings Jefferson Davis to the front.

*   *   *   *   *   *   *   *   *

Mr. Thurman.   I wish to ask the Senator to explain
what he means by bringing Jefferson Davis here?
Does he mean introducing the proposition to pension
soldiers who served in Mexico?

Mr. Blaine.   Yes, the measure you are agitating
brings him here.

Mr Thurman.   Then it is a crime?

Mr. Blaine.   Not a crime at all.   I am not charg-
ing the Senator with a crime, but I resent with some
little feeling that the Senator should look over to this
side of the Chamber and complain that we are taking

some extraordinary course with the name of Jefferson Davis. We do not bring him here. You bear
his mangled remains before us, and then if we do not
happen to view them with the same admiration that
seems to inspire the Senator from Ohio, we are doing
something derogatory to our own dignity and to the
honor of the country, and when the honorable Senator from Mississippi comes to his defense, the first
word he had to speak for Mr. Davis was that he never
counseled insurrection against the Government. I
took the words down.

Mr. Oglesby. Since when?

Mr. Blaine. Since the close of the war. He has
never counseled insurrection! Let us be thankful.
Why should he not pension a man who has shown
such loyalty that he has never counseled insurrection? That is from the Representative of his own
State. I took the words down when he spoke them;
I was amazed; I did not exactly consider the words
of the honorable Senator from Mississippi a wanton
insult to apply to me or anybody else, but I consider
them to be most extraordinary words, that when
pleading the cause of Jefferson Davis at the bar of the
American Senate to be pensioned on its roll of honor,
his personal representative, his associate, his friend,
his follower, commends him to the American people,
because he has been so loyal that he has never counseled insurrection since the war was over.

This is the man brought in here who, according to
the Senator from Mississippi, is to go down to history the peer of Washington and Hampden, fighting
in the same cause, entitled to the same niche in history, inspired by the same patriotic motives, to be
admired for the same self-consecration.

Let me tell the honorable Senator from Mississippi,
that in all the years that I have served in Congress I
have never voluntarily brought the name of Jefferson
Davis before either branch, but I tell him that he is
asking humanity to forget its instincts and patriotism to be changed to crime, before he will find impartial history place Mr. Jefferson Davis anywhere
in the roll that has for its brightest and greatest
names, George Washington and John Hampden.

After Mr. Lamar had replied to this speech, Mr.
Blaine resumed as follows: Why, Mr. President,
does the honorable Senator from Mississippi declare
that the policy of the Government of the United
States, administered as it has been through the Republican party, has been one of intolerance toward
those who were prominent in the war—if I may use
a euphemism, and leave out rebellion—which is offen-
sive to his ears? Do I understand the honorable
Senator to maintain here on this floor that the Government of the United States has been intolerant?
Certainly the Senator does not mean that.

After a colloquy with Mr. Lamar, Mr. Blaine resumed thus:

The Government of the United States never dis-
franchised or put under political disabilities more than
fourteen thousand men in the entire South. Out
of two millions who were in the war it never dis-
franchised over fourteen thousand men. There are
not two hundred left to-day with political disabilities
upon them. There is not one that ever respectfully
or any other way petitioned to be relieved and was
refused. · I know very well what the honorable Senator from Ohio meant, when he said that Hon. Jefferson
Davis should commend himself, because he was not

an office-seeker and had not asked to be relieved of disabilities. Why, if the newspapers are to be credited, especially those in the Southern Democratic interest, Mr. Davis is a candidate for office; he is pledged to sit on the other side of this Chamber two years hence, and the honorable Senator from Ohio will in the next Congress with his eloquence—I am predicting now—urge that these disabilities be removed from him. I predict further that he will urge it without Jefferson Davis paying the respect to the great Government against which he rebelled, simply asking in respectful language that disabilities be taken from him. He has never asked it; I am very sure that another great leader in the South, Mr. Toombs, of Georgia, has boasted that he would never do it. and in the House of Representatives three years ago, when the general amnesty bill was pending and it was proposed that the amnesty should be granted merely on the condition that it should be asked for by each person desiring it, that it was resisted to the bitter end—this great Government was to go to them and ask them if they would take it. The action of the Democratic House of Representatives—I am speaking of the past now, which is quite within parliamentary limits—the action of the Democratic House of Representatives was not that Jefferson Davis might have his disabilities removed upon respectful petition, but that we should go to him and petition him to allow us to remove them.

During the political campaign in the fall of 1878, Mr. Blaine took an active part on the stump, speaking in favor of the financial policy and other public measures of the Republican party.

When the bill to restrict Chinese emigration was

under consideration in the spring of 1879, Mr. Blaine took a decided stand in its favor.

The following speech of Hon. James G. Blaine, of Maine, was delivered in the United States Senate, Monday, April 14, 1879:

[The Senate having under consideration the bill (H. R. No. 1), making appropriations for the support of the Army for the fiscal year ending June 30, 1880, and for other purposes.]

Mr. President: The existing section of the Revised Statutes numbered 2002 reads thus:

No military or naval officer, or other person engaged in the civil, military, or naval service of the United States, shall order, bring, keep or have under his authority or control, any troops or armed men at the place where any general or special election is held in any State unless it be necessary to repel the armed enemies of the United States, *or to keep the peace at the polls.*

The object of the proposed section, which has just been read at the Clerk's desk, is to get rid of the eight closing words, namely, " or to keep the peace at the polls," and therefore the mode of legislation proposed in the Army Bill now before the Senate is an unusual mode; it is an extraordinary mode. If you want to take off a single sentence at the end of a section in the Revised Statutes the ordinary way is to strike off those words, but the mode chosen in this bill is to repeat and re-enact the whole section leaving those few words out. While I do not wish to be needlessly suspicious on a small point, I am quite persuaded that this did not happen by accident, but that it came by design. If I may so speak it came of cunning, the intent being to create the impression that, whereas the Republicans in the administration of the General Government had been using troops right and left, hither and thither, in every direction, as soon as the Democrats got power they enacted this section. I can imagine Democratic candidates for Congress all over the country reading this section to gaping and listening audiences as one of the first offsprings of Democratic reform, whereas every word of it, every syllable of it, from its first to its last, is the enactment of a Republican Congress.

I repeat that this unusual form presents a dishonest issue, whether so intended or not. It presents the issue that as soon as the Democrats got possession of the Federal Government they proceeded to enact the clause which is thus expressed. The law was passed by a Republican Congress in 1865. There were forty-six Senators sitting in this Chamber at the time, of whom only ten or at most eleven were Democrats. The House of Representatives was overwhelmingly Republican. We were in the midst of a war. The Republican Administration had a million, or possibly twelve hundred thousand, bayonets at its command. Thus circumstanced and thus surrounded, with the amplest possible power to interfere with elections had they so designed, with soldiers in every hamlet and county of the United States, the Republican party themselves placed that provision on the statute-book, and Abraham Lincoln, their President, signed it.

I beg you to observe, Mr. President, that this is the first instance in the legislation of the United States, in which any restrictive clause whatever was put upon the statute-book in regard to the use of troops at the polls. The Republican party did it with the Senate and the House in their control. Abraham Lincoln

signed it when he was Commander-in-Chief of an
army larger than ever Napoleon Bonaparte had at his
command. So much by way of correcting an ingeni-
ous and studied attempt at misrepresentation.

The alleged object is to strike out the few words
that authorize the use of troops to keep peace at the
polls. This country has been alarmed, I rather think
indeed amused, at the great effort made to create a
wide-spread impression that the Republican party
relies for its popular strength upon the use of the
bayonet. This Democratic Congress has attempted
to give a bad name to this country throughout the
civilized world, and to give it on a false issue. They
have raised an issue that has no foundation in fact
—that is false in whole and detail, false in the charge,
false in all the specifications. That impression sought
to be created, as I say, not only throughout the North
American continent, but in Europe to-day, is that
elections are attempted in this country to be controlled by the bayonet.

I denounce it here as a false issue. I am not at
liberty to say that any gentleman making the issue
knows it to be false; I hope he does not; but I am
going to prove to him that it is false, and that there
is not a solitary inch of solid earth on which to rest
the foot of any man that makes that issue. I have in
my hand an official transcript of the location and the
number of all the troops of the United States east of
Omaha. By "east of Omaha," I mean all the United
States east of the Mississippi river and that belt of
States that border the Mississippi River on the west,
including forty-one million at least out of the forty-
five million of people that this country is supposed
to contain to-day. In that magnificent area—I will

not pretend to state its extent—but with forty-one million people, how many troops of the United States are there to-day? Would any Senator on the opposite side like to guess, or would he like to state how many men with muskets in their hands there are in the vast area I have named? There are two thousand seven hundred and ninety-seven! And not one more.

From the headwaters of the Mississippi River to the Lakes, and down the great chain of Lakes, and down the Saint Lawrence, and down the valley of the Saint John, and down the Saint Croix, striking the Atlantic Ocean and following it down to Key West, around the Gulf, up to the mouth of the Mississippi again, a frontier of eight thousand miles, either bordering on the ocean or upon foreign territory, is guarded by these troops. Within this domain forty-five fortifications are manned and eleven arsenals protected. There are sixty troops to every million of people. In the South I have the entire number in each State and will give it.

I believe the Senator from Delaware is alarmed, greatly alarmed about the over-riding of the popular ballot by troops of the United States! In Delaware there is not a single armed man, not one. The United States has not even one soldier in the State.

The honorable Senator from West Virginia (Mr. Hereford), on Friday last, lashed himself into a passion, or at least into a perspiration, over the wrongs of his State, trodden down by the iron heel of military despotism. There is not a solitary man of the United States, uniformed, on the soil of West Virginia, and there has not been for years.

In Maryland? I do not know whether my esteemed friend from Maryland (Mr. Whyte) has been greatly alarmed or not; but at Fort McHenry, guarding the entrance to the beautiful harbor of his beautiful city, there are one hundred and ninety-two artillerymen located.

In Virginia. there is a school of practice at Fortress Monroe. My honorable friend (Mr. Withers), who has charge of this bill, knows very well, and if he does not I will tell him, that outside of that school of practice at Fortress Monroe, which has two hundred and eighty-two men in it, there is not a Federal soldier on the soil of Virginia—not one.

North Carolina. Are the Senators from that State alarmed at the immediate and terrible prospect of being over-run by the Army of the United States? On the whole soil of North Carolina there are but thirty soldiers guarding a fort at the mouth of Cape Fear River—just thirty.

South Carolina. I do not see a Senator on the floor from that State. There are one hundred and twenty artillerymen guarding the approaches to Charleston Harbor, and not another soldier on her soil.

Georgia. Does my gallant friend from Georgia (Mr. Gordon) who knows better than I the force and strength of military organization—the senior Senator, and the junior also—are both or either of those Senators alarmed at the presence of twenty-nine soldiers in Georgia? [Laughter] There are just twenty-nine there.

Florida has one hundred and eighty-two at three separate posts, principally guarding the navy yard, near which my friend on the opposite side (Mr. Jones) lives.

Tennessee. Is the honorable Senator from Tennessee (Mr. Bailey) alarmed at the progress of military despotism in his State? There is not a single

Federal soldier on the soil of Tennessee—not one.

Kentucky. I see both the honorable Senators from Kentucky here. They have equal cause with Tennessee to be alarmed, for there is not a Federal soldier in Kentucky—not one!

Missouri. Not one.

Arkansas. Fifty-seven in Arkansas.

Alabama. I think my friend from Alabama (Mr. Morgan) is greatly excited over this question, and in his State there are thirty-two Federal soldiers located at an arsenal of the United States.

Mississippi. The great State of Mississippi. that is in danger of being trodden under the iron hoof of military power, has not a Federal soldier on its soil.

Louisiana has two hundred and thirty-nine.

Texas, apart from the regiments that guard the frontier on the Rio Grande and the Indian frontier. has not one.

And the entire South has eleven hundred and fifty-five soldiers to intimidate, over-run, oppress. and destroy the liberties of fifteen million people! In the Southern States there are twelve hundred and three counties. If you distribute the soldiers there is not quite one for each county; and when I give the counties I give them from the census of 1870. If you distribute them territorially there is one for every seven hundred square miles of territory, so that if you make a territorial distribution. I would remind the honorable Senator from Delaware, if I saw him in his seat, that the quota for his State would be three— "one ragged sergeant and two abreast," as the old song has it. [Laughter.] That is the force ready to destroy the liberties of Delaware!

Mr. PRESIDENT, it was said, as the old maxim has it, that the soothsayers of Rome could not look each other in the face without smiling. There are not two Democratic Senators on this floor who can go into the cloak-room and look each other in the face without smiling at this talk, or, more appropriately, I should say without blushing—the whole thing is such a prodigious and absolute farce, such a miserably manufactured false issue, such a pretense without the slightest foundation in the world, and talked about most and denounced the loudest in States that have not had a single Federal soldier. In New England we have three hundred and eighty soldiers. Throughout the South it does not run quite seventy to the million people. In New England we have absolutely one hundred and twenty soldiers to the million. New England is far more over-run to-day by the Federal soldier, immensely more, than the whole South is. I never heard anybody complain about it in New England, or express any very great fear of their liberties being endangered by the presence of a handful of troops.

As I have said, the tendency of this talk is to give us a bad name in Europe. Republican institutions are looked upon there with jealousy. Every misrepresentation, every slander is taken up and exaggerated and talked about to our discredit, and the Democratic party of the country to-day stands indicted, and I here indict them, for public slander of their country, creating the impression in the civilized world that we are governed by a ruthless military despotism. I wonder how amazing it would be to any man in Europe, familiar as Europeans are with great armies, if he were told that over a territory

larger than France and Spain and Portugal and
Great Britain and Holland and Belgium and the Ger-
man Empire all combined, there were but eleven hundred and fifty-five soldiers! That is all this Democratic howl, this mad cry, this false issue, this absurd
talk is based on—the presence of eleven hundred and
fifty-five soldiers on eight hundred and fifty thousand
square miles of territory, not double the number of
the Democratic police in the city of Baltimore, not a
third of the police in the city of New York, not
double the Democratic police in the city of New
Orleans. I repeat, the number indicts them; it
stamps the whole cry as without any foundation; it
derides the issue as a false and scandalous and partisan make-shift.

What then is the real motive underlying this
movement? Senators on that side. Democratic orators on the stump cannot make any sensible set of
men at the cross-roads believe that they are afraid of
eleven hundred and fifty-five soldiers distributed one
to each county in the South. The minute you state
that, everybody sees the utter, palpable, and laugh-
able absurdity of it, and therefore we must go further
and find a motive for all this cry. We want to find
out, to use a familiar and vulgar phrase, what is "the
cat under the meal." It is not the troops. That is
evident. There are more troops, by fifty per cent.,
scattered through the Northern States east of the
Mississippi to-day than through the Southern States
east of the Mississippi, and yet nobody in the North
speaks of it; everybody would be laughed at for
speaking of it; and therefore the issue, I take no risk
in stating, I make bold to declare, that this issue on
the troops, being a false one, being one without foun-

dation, conceals the true issue, which is simply to get
rid of the Federal presence at Federal elections, to
get rid of the *civil power of the United States* in the
election of Representatives to the Congress of the
United States. That is the whole of it; and, disguise
it as you may, there is nothing else in it or of it.

You simply want to get rid of the supervision by
the Federal Government of the election of Representatives to Congress through civil means; and therefore this bill connects itself directly with another bill,
and you cannot discuss this military bill without discussing a bill which we had before us last winter,
known as the Legislative, Executive, and Judicial Appropriation bill. I am quite well aware, I profess to
be as well aware as any one, that it is not permissible
for me to discuss a bill that is pending before the
other House. I am quite well aware that propriety
and parliamentary rule forbids that I should speak of
what is done in the House of Representatives; but I
know very well that I am not forbidden to speak of
that which is not done in the House of Representatives. I am quite free to speak of the things that are
not done there, and therefore I am free to declare
that neither this Military bill, nor the Legislative, Executive, and Judicial Appropriation bill, ever emanated
from any committee of the House of Representatives
at all; they are not the work of any committee of
the House of Representatives, and, although the
present House of Representatives is almost evenly
balanced in party division, there has been allowed no
solitary suggestion to come from the minority of that
House in regard to the shaping of these bills. Where
do they come from? We are not left to infer; we are
not even left the Yankee privilege of guessing, be-

cause we know. The Senator from Kentucky (Mr. Beck) obligingly told us—I have his exact words here—"that the honorable Senator from Ohio (Mr. Thurman) was the chairman of a committee appointed by the Democratic party to see how it was best to present all these questions before us." Therefore when I discuss these two bills together I am violating no parliamentary law, I am discussing the offspring and the creation of the Democratic caucus, of which the Senator from Ohio, whom I do not see in his seat, is the Chairman.

Mr. WITHERS. I would ask the Senator if this bill was presented to the Senate by the Democratic caucus?

Mr. BLAINE. No, sir.

Mr. WITHERS. I would also ask if it was not reported by the grand Committee of the Whole, the highest committee of all committees, to the House of Representatives by a majority?

Mr. BLAINE. Now you are asking me to tell what the House did. I would not do that. because that is against parliamentary law. [Laughter.]

Mr. WITHERS. It is probably against policy.

Mr. BLAINE. No, against parliamentary law. I will not discuss what the House is doing at all. The Senator cannot lead me into that. When he speaks about its being before a committee here, that is true.

Mr. WITHERS. I wanted merely to say that I do not regard it as an improper suggestion, and in view of the broad declaration made by the Senator from Maine, both as to this bill and the other bill, of which the Senate has no knowledge, but which. I see, he proposes to debate, I cannot blame him for it; I cannot find any objection particularly that he should

drag in another bill in order to hang a speech upon
it. I have no objection to that; but in view of the
declaration that it was not reported by any committee, I simply wished to call attention to the fact that
it was reported by the Committee on Appropriations.

MR. BLAINE. The Senator asked me if it was not
referred to a committee in this branch. Does the
Senator wish me to answer that question, whether
this bill I am discussing before the Senate now was
before the Committee on Appropriations?

MR. WITHERS. The Senator can consult his own
pleasure in regard to the matter.

MR. BLAINE. I suppose the Senator asked me
what was done. I will not speak of what took place
in the Committee on Appropriations, but I think the
Senate can infer what took place there from what
took place in the Senate Chamber last Friday, when
in solid phalanx the other side would not allow even
a grammatical mistake to be corrected; and I repeat
that up to this time no committee of either branch of
Congress has exercised the slightest discretion whatever upon this bill, or been permitted to do so in
either branch of Congress.

MR. WITHERS. I entirely dissent from the statement. Of course, it is not proper for either the Senator or I to disclose what passed in the committee-
room, but I deny utterly the accuracy of the statement.

MR. BLAINE. This bill came from the Democratic
caucus committee. It went to the House of Representatives. What took place there I will not speak
of. It came here; it went into the Committee on
Appropriations of this body. What took place there
I will not speak of; but I know it came back here

without dotting an *i* or crossing a *t*.   If there is any inference to be made——

Mr. Davis, of West Virginia.   I ask the Senator whether he was not on a sub-committee to consider the Army bill, the very bill which he has now in his hand.

Mr. Blaine.   I was a member of that sub-commit. tee.   The honorable Senator, who is chairman of the Appropriations Committee, did me the honor to appoint me upon it; that is true ; and I believe there is no impropriety in my speaking of what a sub-committee did.   We sat on that bill, and we were never permitted to make any change in it whatever, not the slightest in the world.

Mr. Davis, of West Virginia.   Will the Senator tell me why he was not permitted ?

Mr. Blaine.   You ask me the secrets of the Democratic prison-house, why I was not permitted?   I do not know.   That is for you to tell.   I want you to tell me why I was not permitted.

Mr. Withers.   Because you did not have enough support.

Mr. Blaine.   Because I was out-voted.

Mr. Withers.   .That is the whole thing.

Mr. Blaine.   Two to one.

Mr. Withers.   The Senator said no opportunity was offered for any modification or amendment.   It was from that statement I dissented ; and I wish to call his attention to the fact that the broad way in which he has stated it cannot be sustained by the facts within his own knowledge.

Mr. Blaine.   Now I really get at the point made by the Senator.

Mr. Withers.   The majority only exercised that

control over the bill which they have always the right to do.

Mr. Blaine. The Senator has told so much now that he really forces me to tell more, and that more is, that when I offered several amendments in the sub-committee they said, "we really agree to these, and if we permit the bill to be altered at all we will let these in, but we do not intend to let this bill be touched." That was what was said in our committee. They did not object to several suggestions I made in regard to amendments to the bill, but they simply sat and voted me down. This is the reason why I could not amend it.

Now, Mr. President, I say you cannot possibly debate one of these bills without debating the other, because when you come to read this new section 2002 in the military bill, it is to prevent any civil officer of the United States being present on election day. I am not now talking about military officers; there is not a Senator on that side of the Chamber who ever saw a military force at the polls, in my judgment.

Mr. Withers. The Senator is mistaken.

Mr. Hereford. I desire to say in that connection—

The Vice-President. Does the Senator from Maine yield?

Mr. Blaine. I will yield for testimony on that point.

Mr. Hereford. The Senator, in making the assertion that he has made, is not only assuming to himself the power of omniscience, but ubiquity, that he at all times has been at all the polls—

Mr. Blaine. Do not delay on that.   Tell me if you ever saw anybody there?

MR. HEREFORD. Yes, sir.

MR. BLAINE. That is what I want to know.

MR. HEREFORD. Prior to the time that the State of West Virginia passed from under the control of the Republican party we always had the military there, and I have seen them at the polls making arrests on the day of voting in my own town.

MR. BLAINE. When?

MR. HEREFORD. When?

MR. BLAINE. Yes, when did you ever see a military man in the uniform of the United States making arrests at the polls?

MR. HEREFORD. I have known of them making arrests in Mercer County.

MR. BLAINE. When?

MR. HEREFORD. If you stop a moment, I can look back and think.

MR. BLAINE. I want to know when?

MR. HEREFORD. In 1870, sir.

MR. BLAINE. Ten years ago?

MR. HEREFORD. About that.

MR. BLAINE. Or before that?

MR. HEREFORD. It was after the war. I saw this: We had a company of soldiers stationed in the town where I lived, within one hundred steps of the voting place, and that company on day of election were divided up, a part of them sent to an adjoining county—the county of Mercer—where they expected to control the voters.

MR. BLAINE. One company?

MR. HEREFORD. And were placed there within seventy yards of the place of voting.

Mr. BLAINE. What did they arrest anybody for?

MR. HEREFORD. For the purpose of intimidation.

Mr. Blaine.   Oh, yes!

Mr. Hereford,   For the purpose of intimidation.

Mr. Blaine.   I should be glad to hear any other testimony on that side.

Mr. Williams.   I can tell the honorable Senator that I saw soldiers marched into the public square and stack their arms since the war.

Mr. Blaine.   What time since the war.

Mr. Williams.   Eighteen hundred and sixty-five.

Mr. Blaine.   That is a good while ago, and Kentucky was in a condition of upheaval about that time, 1865.

Mr. Williams.   And I know from information that they were stationed at a number of polls in other portions of the State.

Mr. Blaine.   Has the Senator seen any since that time?

Mr. Williams.   This I saw with my own eyes.   I saw men go up in the presence of soldiers to vote.

Mr. Blaine.   Has the Senator seen any since 1865?

Mr. Williams.   No, sir.

Mr. Blaine.   The Senator then has had fourteen years to brood over that, and he cannot stand it a minute longer.

Mr. Williams.   The power to put them there is still in the law; and it is to deprive the President of the authority to take them to the polls for which we now contend.

Mr. Blaine.   The Senator tells us that he is particularly sensitive about what he saw when the country was still in a disturbed condition, fourteen years ago, while to-day there is not, and has not been for years, a solitary Federal soldier in Kentucky—not one. That is his testimony. Has any other Senator a statement to make?

MR. WITHERS. The Senator will recollect that he denied that any Senator on this side of the Chamber had ever seen a soldier at the polls.

MR. BLAINE. No; I queried it; I did not deny it.

MR. WITHERS. I understood the Senator to make the statement broadly.

MR. BLAINE. I was not so broadly ubiquitous as the honorable Senator from West Virginia supposed. I wanted to know whether any Senator there would rise up and say he had seen it.

MR. WITHERS. I am willing to abide by the reporter's record of the remarks of the Senator.

MR. BLAINE. If I made a slip of the tongue I will gladly correct it. I could not be at every polling place in the South. There are thirteen thousand polling places in the South, and there are eleven hundred and fifty-five soldiers down there, and this great intimidation is to be carried on by one soldier distributing himself around to twelve polling places. That is the intimidation that threatens the South just now; and I am just reminded by the honorable Senator from Wisconsin (Mr. Carpenter) that the Supreme Court decided—a fact I did not recall at the moment—that the war did not close till April, 1866; a state of peace had not come, and therefore the honorable Senator from Kentucky does not bring himself within the line of evidence. He only saw troops there in 1865, during the war. Has he seen them since April, 1866, in time of peace?

MR. WILLIAMS. No.

MR. BLAINE. He has not. [Laughter.] Then

should like some other Senator, if there is any one that has testimony to give; I should like to see some other Senator that has seen troops around the polls, bull-dozing and brow-beating and intimidating and controlling the popular wish, to rise if he has any testimony to give on the subject.

MR. LOGAN. If the Senator will allow me, perhaps I can make a statement about soldiers in Kentucky in 1865 myself. I happened to be in Louisville in 1865 at the time of an election for Congress, when General Rousseau was a candidate for Representative in Congress. I was stationed at Louisville and had sixty-five thousand soldiers under my command. I was there on the day of election, and I made a speech there the night before the election. Those sixty-five thousand soldiers were stationed all around Louisville, and I never saw a more quiet, peaceable election in my life, and under orders the soldiers were kept from the polls and out of the city during the day of the election, under my own orders.

MR. BLAINE. All we get, then, in the testimony is, that the Senator from Kentucky says he saw troops in his State during the war, and the Senator from West Virginia says he saw them in his State once since the war—ten years ago. That is the amount of actual testimony we get on the subject. Now, Mr. President, I say this bill connects itself directly with the provisions which are inserted by the Democratic caucus in the Legislative, Executive, and Judicial bill. The two stand together: they cannot be separated; because to-day if we enact that no civil officer whatever shall appear under any circumstances with armed men at the polls—I am not speaking of Federal troops or military or naval officers—I should like to know how, if you strike that out to-day in the military bill that is pending, you are going to enforce any provisions of the Election Laws, even if we leave them standing. Take this section of the Election Law, section 2024 of the Revised Statutes:

The marshal or his general deputies, or such special deputies as are thereto specially empowered by him, in writing, and under his hand and seal, whenever he, or either, or any of them, is forcibly resisted in executing their duties under this title, or shall, by violence, threats, or menaces, be prevented from executing such duties, or from arresting any person who has committed any offense for which the marshal or his general or his special deputies are authorized to make such arrest, are, and each of them is, empowered to summon and call to his aid the bystanders or *posse comitatus* of his district.

I should like any one to tell me whether a marshal can call together armed men under that, if you repeal this section in the Military bill? Under heavy penalties, you say that no civil officer whatever, no matter what the disturbances, at an election of Representatives to Congress — no civil officer of the United States shall keep order. You do not say that in that same election the State officer may not be there with all the force he chooses, legal or illegal. You say that the United States, in an election which specially concerns the Federal Government, shall not have anything whatever to do with it. That is what you say, although the Constitution, as broadly as language can express it, gives the Government of the United States, if it chooses to exercise it, the absolute control of the whole subject—familiar to schoolboys who have even once read the Constitution, in the clause: "The times, places, and manner of hold-

9

ing elections for Senators and Representatives shall be prescribed in each State by the Legislature thereof; but the Congress may at any time, by law, make or alter such regulations, except as to the places of choosing Senators." And every one knows that the contemporaneous exposition of that part of the Constitution, familiar also to every one in the country, the exposition by Madison and Hamilton, was to the effect that "every government ought to contain in itself the means of its own preservation;" and according to Mr. Madison, quoting a Southern authority, it was "more consonant to just theories to intrust the Union with the care of its own existence than to transfer that care to any other hands."

There is not the slightest possible denial here that this is a constitutional exercise of power. If there is such a denial it is a mere individual opinion. There has been no adjudication in the least degree looking to the unconstitutionality of these laws. Your individual opinion is no better than mine; mine is no better than that of any other man who can hear a horn blown from the front steps of the Capitol. No individual opinion is worth anything. We have a department of the Government to pass upon the question. The legislative department has enacted these laws under what it believed to be a clear and explicit grant of power, and you have never had it judicially determined otherwise. But now you propose to assault the Election Laws, the supervisors, and the marshals in this Military bill; and under the pretense of getting rid of troops at the polls you propose that no Federal officer—no civil officer of the Federal Government—shall be there. That is the design; that is the plain, palpable object. An amendment that will be offered here will test your sincerity on that subject; whether you will allow the Federal Government to be present at all. I believe you do propose to allow two men of straw to stand up without any power; to be present as witnesses; to be counted themselves but not to count, as my friend from Massachusetts (Mr. Hoar) well suggests; with no power whatever; mere spectators on sufferance, not to be hustled out, nor kicked, nor clubbed, if they behave themselves, but entirely at the mercy of the mob—guests standing there by the courtesy of the State, not standing there armed with the panoply of the Federal Government and commanding in its great name an observance of law and of justice. You propose simply to permit, and permit is the word, two officers to be designated by Federal authority to be present, that is all; not to have one particle of power, not to be clothed with a solitary attribute of authority, not to have any force, not to have any legal status beyond that of casual spectators; and, therefore, I say that you cannot debate this question without associating these two bills together. The one runs right into the other; and I go so far as to say that if the Military bill should go through in its present form and become the law of the land, the remainder of this law on election day is not worth anything at all. The whole law of marshals and supervisors is worth nothing unless the civil authority of the United States has the power there to enforce its edicts.

We are told too, rather a novel thing, that if we do not take these laws, we are not to have the appropriations. I believe it has been announced in both branches of Congress, I suppose on the authority of the Democratic caucus, that if we do not take these

bills as they are planned, we shall not have any of
the appropriations that go with them.   The honorable
Senator from West Virginia (Mr. Hereford) told it
to us on Friday; the honorable Senator from Ohio
(Mr. Thurman) told it to us last session; the honor-
orable Senator from Kentucky (Mr. Beck) told it to
us at the same time, and I am not permitted to speak
of the legions who told us so in the other House. They
say all these appropriations are to be refused—not
merely the Army appropriation, for they do not stop
at that.   Look, for a moment, at the Legislative bill
that came from the Democratic caucus.   Here is an
appropriation in it for defraying the expenses of the
Supreme Court and the Circuit and District Courts
of the United States, including the District of Colum-
bia, &c., "$2,800,000:" " Provided,"—provided what?

That the following sections of the Revised Statutes relating
to elections—

Going on to recite them—

be repealed.

That is, you will pass an appropriation for the support of the Judiciary of the United States only on
condition of this repeal.   We often speak of this
Government being divided between three great departments, the executive, the legislative, and the judicial—
co-ordinate, independent, equal.   The legislative, under the control of a Democratic caucus, now steps
forward and says : " We offer to the Executive this
bill, and if he does not sign it we are going to starve
the Judiciary."   That is carrying the thing a little
further than I have ever known.   We do not merely
propose to starve the Executive if he will not sign
the bill, but we propose to starve the Judiciary that
has had nothing whatever to do with the question.

That has been boldly avowed on this floor; that has been boldly avowed in the other House; that has been boldly avowed in Democratic papers throughout the country.

And you propose not merely to starve the Judiciary, but you propose that you will not appropriate a solitary dollar to take care of this Capitol. The men who take care of this great amount of public property are provided for in that bill. You say they shall not have any pay if the President will not agree to change the Election Laws. There is the public printing that goes on for the enlightenment of the whole country and for printing the public documents of every one of the Departments. You say they shall not have a dollar for public printing unless the President agrees to repeal these laws.

There is the Congressional Library that has become the pride of the whole American people for its magnificent growth and extent. You say it shall not have one dollar to take care of it, much less add a new book, unless the President signs these bills. There is the Department of State that we think throughout the history of the Government has been a great pride to this country for the ability with which it has conducted our foreign affairs; it is also to be starved. You say we shall not have any intercourse with foreign nations, not a dollar shall be appropriated therefor unless the President signs these bills. There is the Light-House Board that provides for the beacons and the warnings on seventeen thousand miles of sea and gulf and lake coast. You say those lights shall all go out, and not a dollar shall be appropriated for the board, if the President does not sign these bills. There are the mints of the United States at Philadelphia, New Orleans, Denver, San Francisco, coining silver and coining gold—not a dollar shall be appropriated for them if the President does not sign these bills. There is the Patent Office, the patents issued which embody the invention of the country—not a dollar for them. The Pension Bureau shall cease its operations unless these bills are signed and patriotic soldiers may starve. The Agricultural Bureau, the Post-Office Department, every one of the great executive functions of the Government is threatened, taken by the throat, highwayman-style, collared on the highway, commanded to stand and deliver in the name of the Democratic Congressional caucus. That is what it is; simply that. No committee of this Congress in either branch has ever recommended that legislation—not one. Simply a Democratic caucus has done it.

Of course this is new. We are learning something every day. I think you may search the records of the Federal Government in vain; it will take some one much more industrious in that search than I have ever been, and much more observant than I have ever been, to find any possible parallel or any sensible suggestion in our past history of any such thing. Most of the Senators who sit in this Chamber can remember some vetoes by Presidents that shook this country to its centre with excitement. The veto of the National-Bank bill by Jackson in 1832, remembered by the oldest in this Chamber; the veto of the National-Bank bill in 1841 by Tyler, remembered by those not the oldest, shook this country with a political excitement which up to that time had scarcely a parallel; and it was believed, whether rightfully or wrongfully is no matter—it was believed by those who advocated those financial measures at the time, that they were of the very last importance to the well-being and prosperity of the people of the Union. That was believed by the great and shining lights of that day. It was believed by that man of imperial character and imperious will, the great Senator from Kentucky. It was believed by Mr. Webster, the greatest of New England Senators. When Jackson vetoed the one or Tyler vetoed the other, did you ever hear a suggestion that those bank charters should be put on appropriation bills, or that there should not be a dollar to run the Government until they were signed? So far from it that, in 1841, when temper was at its height; when the Whig party, in addition to losing their great measure, lost it under the sting and the irritation of what they believed was a desertion by the President whom they had chosen; and when Mr. Clay, goaded by all these considerations, rose to debate the question in the Senate, he repelled the suggestion of William C. Rives, of Virginia, who attempted to make upon him the point that he had indulged in some threat involving the independence of the Executive. Mr. Clay rose to his full height and thus responded :

"I said nothing whatever of any obligation on the part of the President to conform his judgment to the opinions of the Senate and House of Representatives, although the Senator argued as if I had, and persevered in so arguing after repeated correction. I said no such thing. I know and I respect the perfect independence of each department, acting within its proper sphere, of the other departments."

A leading Democrat, an eloquent man, a man who has courage and frankness and many good qualities, has boasted publicly that the Democracy are in power

for the first time in eighteen years, and they do not
intend to stop until they have wiped out every vestige
of every war measure. Well, "forewarned is fore-
armed," and you begin appropriately on a measure
that has the signature of Abraham Lincoln. I think
the picture is a striking one, when you hear these
words from a man who was then in arms against the
Government of the United States, doing his best to
destroy it, exerting every power given him in a bloody
and terrible rebellion against the authorty of the
United States, and when Abraham Lincoln was marching at the same time to his martyrdom in its defense!
Strange times have fallen upon us, that those of us
who had the great honor to be associated in higher or
lower degree with Mr. Lincoln, in the administration
of the Government, should live to hear men in public
life and on the floors of Congress, fresh from the bat-
tle-fields of the rebellion, threatening the people of
the United States that the Democratic party, in power
for the first time in eighteen years, proposes not to
stay its hand until every vestige of the war measures
has been wiped out! The late Vice-President of the
Confederacy boasted—perhaps I had better say stated
—that for sixty out of the seventy-two years preceding the outbreak of the rebellion, from the foundation
of the Government, the South, though in a minority,
had, by combining with what he termed the anti-cen-
tralists in the North, ruled the country; and in 1866
the same gentleman indicated in a speech, I think
before the Legislature of Georgia, that by a return to
Congress the South might repeat the experiment with
the same successful result. I read that speech at the
time; but I little thought I should live to see so near
a fulfillment of its prediction. I see here to-day two

great measures emanating, as I have said, not from a committee of either House, but from a Democratic caucus in which the South has an overwhelming majority, two-thirds in the House, and out of the forty-two Senators on the other side of this Chamber, professing the Democratic faith, thirty are from the South— twenty-three, a positive and pronounced majority, having themselves been participants in the war against the Union, either in military or civil station. So that is a matter of fact, plainly deducible from counting your fingers, the legislation of this country to-day, shaped and fashioned in a Democratic caucus where the Confederates of the South hold the majority, is the realization of Mr. Stephens' prophecy. And, very appropriately, the House under that control and the Senate under that control, embodying thus the entire legislative powers of the Government, deriving its political strength from the South, elected from the South, say to the President of the United States, at the head of the Executive Department of the Government, elected as he was from the North—elected by the whole people, but elected as a Northern man; elected on Republican principles, elected in opposition to the party that controls both branches of Congress to-day—they naturally say, " You shall not exercise your Constitutional power to veto a bill."

Some gentlemen may rise and say, " Do you call it revolution to put an amendment on an appropriation bill?" Of course not. There have been a great many amendments put on appropriation bills, some mischievous and some harmless; but I call it the audacity of revolution for any Senator or Representative, or any caucus of Senators or Representatives, to get together and say, " We will have this legislation or

we will stop the great departments of the Government." That is revolutionary. I do not think it will
amount to revolution; my opinion is it will not. I
think that is a revolution that will not go around;
I think that is a revolution which will not revolve; I
think that is a revolution whose wheel will not turn;
but it is a revolution if persisted in, and if not persisted in, it must be backed out from with ignominy.
The Democratic party in Congress have put themselves exactly in this position to-day, that if they go
forward in the announced programme, they march to
revolution. I think they will, in the end, go back in
an ignominious retreat. That is my judgment.

The extent to which they control the legislation of
the country is worth pointing out. In round numbers,
the Southern people are about one-third of the population of the Union. I am not permitted to speak
of the organization of the House of Representatives,
but I can refer to that of the last House. In the last
House of Representatives, of the forty-two standing
committees the South had twenty-five. I am not blam-
ing the honorable Speaker for it. He was hedged in by
partisan forces, and could not avoid it. In this very
Senate, out of the thirty-four standing committees
the South has twenty-two. I am not calling these
things up just now in reproach; I am only showing
what an admirable prophet the late Vice-President of
the Southern Confederacy was, and how entirely true
all his words have been, and how he has lived to see
them realized.

I do not profess to know, Mr. President, least of
all Senators on this floor, certainly as little as any
Senator on this floor, do I profess to know, what the
President of the United States will do when these

bills are presented to him, as I suppose in due course of time they will be.   I certainly should never speak a solitary word of disrespect of the gentlemen holding that exalted position, and I hope I should not speak a word unbefitting the dignity of the office of a Senator of the United States: But as there has been speculation here and there on both sides as to what he would do, it seems to me that the dead heroes of the Union would rise from their graves, if he should consent to be intimidated and outraged in his proper Constitutional power by threats like these.

All the war measures of Abraham Lincoln are to be wiped out, say leading Democrats!   The Bourbons of France busied themselves, I believe, after the Restoration in removing every trace of Napoleon's power and grandeur, even chiseling the " N " from public monuments raised to perpetuate his glory ; but the dead man's hand from Saint Helena reached out and destroyed them in their pride and in their folly. And I tell the Senators on the other side of this Chamber—I tell the Democratic party North and South—South in the lead and North following—that the slow, unmoving finger of scorn, from the tomb of the martyred President on the prairies of Illinois, will wither and destroy them.   " Though dead he speaketh."   [Great applause in the galleries.]

The PRESIDING OFFICER (MR. ANTHONY in the chair) : The Sergeant-at-Arms will preserve order in the galleries, and arrest persons manifesting approbation or disapprobation.

MR. BLAINE.   When you present these bills with these threats to the living President, who bore the commission of Abraham Lincoln, and served with honor in the Army of the Union, which Lincoln restored and preserved, I can think only of one appropriate response from his lips or his pen. He should say to you with all the scorn befitting his station :

Is thy servant a dog that he should do this thing?

During the political campaign in Ohio, in the Fall of 1879, Mr. Blaine took an active part, and his political tour through the State was much like a triumphal march. Great enthusiasm and enormous audiences greeted him in every portion of the State. His own cousin, Thomas Ewing, was the Democratic candidate for Governor. Mr. Blaine labored actively and earnestly for the election of Charles Foster, the Republican candidate, who was elected by a large majority. During the same Fall Mr. Blaine made a lengthy speech to a meeting of New York merchants, in Cooper Institute, speaking in support of the financial policy and leading measures of the Republican party. The following is Mr. Blaine's speech on this occasion:

MR. CHAIRMAN : It is a healthful and encouraging sign in the politics of the country, when the merchants and business men of the great commercial emporium of the Nation see fit, in their distinctive character, to take part on the Republican side. [Applause.] I thank them for the honor of being permitted to address them. But I shall not apologize because this is a mere State election. The Democrats have been busy in the last month issuing pronunciamentos warning off all outsiders from taking any part in this contest. [Laughter and applause.] Having a disturbance in their own happy family (laughter), and having summoned the National Committee of the Democratic party, embracing one man from every State in the Union, and then having summoned the Hon. Benjamin Hill, of Georgia (laughter and applause mingled with hisses,) as generalissimo in the great task of composing the Democratic troubles of the New York Democracy, in order that they might get into line for the great national contest next year—but these consultations over all the States and Territories in the Union having utterly failed to produce an adjustment, it then occurred to *The New York World*, and other organs of the Democratic party, that this was purely a State contest, (laughter) involving something about your canals and the rate of taxation which the County Supervisors shall levy. Well, if it were only that I should not be here. When Voltaire visited Congreve, the English poet said to him that he preferred to be visited as an English gentleman, and the French wit replied to him, that as an English gentleman he should not have paid the slightest attention to him in the world. [Laughter and applause.] And I am very frank to say that if the question before the people of New York was the rate of taxation to be levied by your County Supervisors, or the amount of cheese-paring which had been affected, or the money that had been saved under the administration of Governor Robinson, I should not be here. But this election has a far wider and far greater and a far grander significance. And I beg you, not only in the specific instance of New York, but generally do observe whenever a hard-pressed or an assistant Democrat (laughter and applause) like Lucius Robinson, of New York, or Benjamin F. Butler, of Massachusetts, (laughter) gets into tight place, they are always sure to make loud proclamation that there is nothing in the world involved but a little penny-whistle State issue, and they warn the people not to take any part in the issue at all.

The Republican party are dealing with weighty
things. They remember that in the Congressional
elections of last year, the Democratic party throughout the country, in combination with the Greenback
party, stood shoulder to shoulder in opposition to the
resumption of specie payments. They remember
that both those parties proclaimed specie payment on
the 1st of January, 1879, as an impossibility. They
remember that they not only proclaimed it as an impossibility, but they said that the Republicans who
were advocating it knew it to be an impossibility and
were engaged in a gigantic conspiracy to deceive the
people. And thus the contest of 1878 closed. The
ancient monarch said, "Time and I against the world."
And so the Republicans had nothing to do but to
wait, and in the revolving seasons the 1st day of January was reached. The 1st day of January was
reached in the year of grace 1879, and then against
all the predictions of the enemies of the Republican
party, on that great day, forever memorable in the
financial history of America, on that great day the
$700,000,000 of paper money in the United States, in
the twinkling of an eye, without commotion, or disturbance, or excitement, was raised to par with coin.
[Applause.] And there it will remain until long after
the death of the great-grandchild of the youngest
person here present. And this generation are permitted to see what no other generation of Americans
ever saw, what no other generation of Americans
ever dared to hope for, a paper currency good everywhere, the same everywhere, good in thirty-eight
States and nine Territories, over 3,000,000 square
miles of area, among 47,000,000 of people, and good
far out and beyond that, good in distant nations and

far-off continents; for while we are here discussing political issues which involve, in a certain sense, the approval of the return of specie payments, while we are here debating and discussing, the Greenback dollar of the United States and the National bank dollar alike are the representatives of coin wherever commerce extends or civilization is known. You can pass them in Liverpool, in London, in Paris, in Vienna, in St. Petersburg, in Cairo, in Bombay, in Hong Kong, in Honolulu, in Melbourne, on all continents and on all islands; and to-night the limit of the circulation and the credit of the paper money of the United States is only that for which the pious old deacon, in the Presbyterian Church, in the monthly concert of prayer for the spread of the Gospel prayed —that the glad tidings of salvation might be carried to the uttermost parts of the earth, even to those desolate regions where the foot of man never trod and the eye of man never saw.

And now there is not in the United States a party that could rise up to destroy the Resumption Act. There is not a party in the United States of sufficient respectability in point of strength to carry a single county that will incorporate in its platform the repeal of the Resumption Act. You may fill a Congress with Benjamin F. Butlers and Samuel J. Tildens and Solon Chases—taking them in a descending scale —and they won't dare repeal the Resumption Act! You can't make a Congress of the United States to-day, selected outside of a lunatic asylum, that would repeal the Resumption Act, and if one Congress should be found that would do it, the people of the United States would rise up with one voice and send them inside the lunatic asylum pretty quickly.

[Laughter.] Therefore, on that great issue, the strong
initial point, the conclusion, really, of the whole controversy, the Republican party stands to-day vindicated and triumphant. And all these opinions, too,
on the financial question, simply nibble round the
edges, and take up some subordinate issue, and try to
excite prejudice, and mislead the people by misstate-
ment of fact. And with great unanimity, eminent
men and men who are not eminent—Senators and
men so little eminent I shall not mention them—jump
with singular unanimity upon the bait, and hold up
the Republican party as guilty of the error, or rather
crime, of establishing a system of banks in this country which are at war with the principles of justice
and with the interests of the people. Now, Mr.
Chairman, I am quite willing to admit—and I am not
going to inflict a discussion on banking upon you—I
am quite willing to admit whatever defect—if defect
there be—exists in the National banking system,
which is chargeable upon the Republican party, I
only ask for a fair debtor and creditor account on the
political ledger, and that whatever of merit there may
be there shall be carried to our account.

When the war broke out we had thirty-three kinds
of paper currency in this country, with the Territories to hear from. [Laughter.] Some was bad, some
was good, and a good deal was indifferent. [Renewed
laughter.] In New York you had good paper currency. It was secured under a certain form and was
in a certain measure the forerunner of the National
system. We thought we had a good system of currency in New England, which we called the Suffolk
banking system. We thought we enjoyed one down
in Maine, and yet regularly—with a periodicity which

beat the return of the equinoctial storm—these banks would turn out defunct. I remember as if it were yesterday, on a pleasant morning in 1858, a large bank in Maine, known as the Shipbuilders' Bank, was announced as failed with $357,000 circulation out—and it is out yet. [Laughter.] There was that good thing about the old State Bank, when it failed it made a clean bang-up. You remember before the war there was a story current in the papers of a celebrated coroner's inquest held on the body of a negro boy in Mississippi. They quit holding coroners' inquests on negroes down there now (laughter) —but then they had value. Well, they had the coroner's inquest on the negro boy, who was found dead in a swamp, though all that was left of him was his skin. After hearing testimony for three days they unanimously returned a verdict of " Found empty." [Laughter.] And that was the verdict on all the old State banks. And every twenty years from the time Washington was inaugurated down to the time of Lincoln, every twenty years the State bank circulation in this country was completely lost, and it wasn't the banks that lost it either. [Laughter.] It was the bill-holders among the people.

Andrew Jackson goes down to history for his uncompromising resistance to, and his ultimate destruction of a great monopoly known as the United States Bank. Whatever politics I have I inherited from the Whig side of the house, and yet I believe in the impartial verdict of history—that the American people believe to-day, and will still more come to believe, that in that contest between Jackson and the United States Bank, Jackson was right and the Whigs were wrong; on this simple ground, that the Congress of

10

the United States ought not and should not have
given to one set of men any particular privilege of
banking over and above any other set of men. [Ap-
plause.] And therefore Jackson crushed it. But
the time had not arrived, the opportunity had not yet
come for Jackson to seize the old State banks.

It would be a rash man who would say that Jackson did not have the courage to seize that system.
He had courage enough for anything, but the time
had not then come. And there never did come a
time when courage and opportunity fell together until
the Republican party came into power; and the Republican party was the first party that ever had the
courage to take hold of the State bank system by the
nape of the neck and hold it over the gulf of financial
perdition, and let it drop down into it. But they did.
They said hereafter in this country there should be
no special charter; they said that hereafter in this
country whatever money there was should be National, that it should not be limited or circumscribed
by State lines. [Applause.] In the olden time I could
not have travelled through ten States, as I have done,
without having to change my money ten times. Why,
if any man had appeared down in Maine before the
war and brought a bill from the State of Ohio or Illinois, to a merchant, the first thing he would have
done would have been to look at his counterfeit de-
tector, and then straightway send for a policeman
(laughter) on the evident presumption that the man
had been either engaged in robbing a bank or utter-
ing counterfeit money.

But the Republican party put an end to that. They
said that money should be National, and when they
came to establish a banking system, they said that

two things should distinguish it. In the first place
it should be just as free to one man in the United
States as to any other, and no man should have a
particle of advantage over any other man. I made
this statement in a public meeting a little while ago,
and a Greenbacker said, " Well "—he jumped up in
the audience, as the Greenbackers used to do very
lively before the election—" Well," said he, " you cannot bank without the bonds." Said I, " Does that
constitute a monopoly in National banking?" " Certainly," he replied, " you confine it to the fellows that
have the bonds." I said, " Did it ever occur to you
that farming was a monopoly?" " Certainly not."
" Well, but it is entirely confined to the fellows who
have the ground. [Laughter.] You cannot farm in
a balloon [renewed laughter] or out at sea in a boat."

The Republican party said that banks should be
open to all alike, and to all on the same terms ; and
then the Republican party, speaking through the instrumentality of National legislation, said this one
great thing—that while banking should be open to
everybody on precisely the same terms, nobody
should issue a solitary dollar of circulating money
until they had put up United States bonds for every
dollar bill, and then they might go, if they chose, and
destroy their bank, they might go and misconduct
themselves, and when they did and their banks, in the
strong language of the " boys," were " bust," the
United States should step forward and sell their
bonds, and take care of the innocent third party,
which is the public. [Applause.] And from that day,
Mr. Chairman, and I beg your attention to this as a
merchant of New York—from that day there has
been no bad money in the United States. [Applause.]

The Republican party abolished bad money; and
from that day forward, whatever money has been issued, has been issued under the image and the super-
scription of the United States.

"Ah! but," says our Greenback friend, "what
do you want any banks to issue at all for; why don't
you have an issue directly from the Government?
What do you want of the instrumentality and the in-
termediate power of the banks to issue for, when you
could do it direct?" Well, that is a wiser question
than they ask in some of their discussions. That is
a question that cannot be passed lightly by. That is
a question demanding an answer, and if it can have
an answer it must be given; if not, the question must
be conceded. Well, I answer that question, being a
Yankee—by adoption at least—I answer that question
with the privilege of a Yankee by asking another, and
to that question I have never been able to get an
answer. And that simple question is: If you propose to have the Government of the United States
issue all the paper money, to whom will you confine
the power of determining the when and how much?
You never saw one of the Greenback resolutions in
your life that didn't say they wanted enough for the
demands of trade and for the business needs of the
country. That is all right. We are all agreed upon
that. We ought to have enough currency in this
country for the demands of trade and the needs of
business; but that is only restating the conundrum.
Who is to determine what shall be the amount needed
for the demands of trade and for the needs of business? And if you have asked that question, as I have
very many times, of very many audiences, and asked
it for an answer, you find that they prefer to reply in

this very way: Why, to be sure, leave it to Congress, leave it to Congress! Well, I am not presumptuous enough to present myself as one knowing a bit more than my neighbor, but I do know a good deal more about Congress than those who have not been there. [Applause.] And I say, there is not a body of men in the United States so utterly unfitted for that function as the Congress of the United States. [Applause.] I say, moreover, that if that function was committed to Congress, there is not a merchant of intelligence—many of whom I have the honor to address —who would have agreed to buy or sell six months ahead, to deliver or sell ten thousand dollars worth of any commodity in the market, with a pending session of Congress that might ruinously contract the currency in one direction, or still more ruinously expand it in the other.

But Congress did perform that function, say the Greenbackers. I would like to know when it was that Congress undertook to decide how much paper currency should be used for the demands of business and trade in this country. "Why, during the war," they said. Why, my Greenback friend, in your infancy in knowledge, when Congress issued greenbacks, the question was not how much money was needed for the business of the country, but whether we were going to have any country left to do business in (laughter and applause)—a still more, a far more important question—and that question was so important that it so entirely over-rode and kept out of view the other, that we issued greenbacks without the slightest possible regard to their effect upon the business of the country. To such a degree was this done that with $150,000,000 of them out they were worth $147,000,000 in gold coin in June, 1862, and with $400,000,000 of them out in June, 1864, they were only worth $145,000,000 in gold coin. If we had kept on in that line, I leave it to the younger portion of my audience to cipher what might have been the result.

But still another and graver point. When the second period arrived, when $400,000,000 of United States greenbacks were worth but $145,000,000 in gold or silver coin, we stood on the eve of what happily proved the closing year of the war. And the Loan bill reported from the Committee of Ways and Means in the XXXVIIIth Congress proposed to borrow from our own people and from whomsoever else would lend it $1,000,000,000. I am recalling to those who have frosted heads facts as familiar to them as to myself. I hope I am reviving to, and possibly teaching, some history to those who were but children and boys at that period. A little while after, the children of that day heard with perfect amazement that the great German Empire in the contest with France, having overthrown the Government of Napoleon, had de-manded the enormous and incalculable indemnity of $1,000,000,000, and it seemed to them an incalculable sum indeed. But yet when we stood on the eve of the fourth year of the war, we had already spent on the average a thousand million of dollars in each of the three preceeding years, and we were proposing to borrow a thousand million for the fourth, and as a matter of fact we actually spent $1,300,000,000. Do you ever reflect what it is to belong to a country that spends $1,300,000,000 a year? When Congress stood at this critical point in the history of the country, they realized, as every man of sense outside of Congress realized, that the destruction of the greenback was the destruction of the National credit of the United States. [Applause.]

There has been a great deal of "bosh"—if I may use that term—a great deal of "bosh" talked about the difference between the bondholder and the greenbackholder. Every man of sense knows, or he ought to know, that there never was a moment in the financial ial history of the United States when the greenback could have been destroyed without carrying the bonds down with them. Never. When the Continental currency ceased to be of value every other form of currency went down; and there never was a moment when Congress could have permitted the greenback to have been sacrificed without sacrificing every other form of National credit. Congress understood that, and when they framed the great closing Loan bill of the war, they put it there voluntarily—I ought not to put that word in; thank God, the United States have never been forced to do anything. [Laughter and applause.] Of course they did it voluntarily; they put it in the forefront of the bill that the total amount of United States notes—that is greenbacks—issued and to be issued, should never exceed $400,000,000. And that in the forefront of the closing Loan bill, which furnished the money for the great and victorious campaigns of Grant and Sherman (applause), constituted as solemn and as honorable a pledge as a great people could give. The people of the United States stood—if you might personify them in one man—before the nations of the world and before their own people; they said: "We have a great country here; it spans a continent; its authority is resisted by a wicked and causeless rebellion. We ask you to loan us the money to supply the men and means to put that rebellion down; and lest you may have any fear that the currency of the country shall be destroyed, and its bonds thereby destroyed also, we agree herewith to give you, in this hour of need, to be sacredly observed in the hour of triumph—we give you that undivided pledge of a great people, that the greenback currency of this country shall never exceed $400,000,000." And for that declaration every Democrat in the Senate and every Democrat in the House voted with every Republican in the Senate and every Republican in the House. The vote was unanimous, unanimous.

Now, what a man may do ignorantly, may God forgive him! But a man that voted for that, and has, in his own witness, seen the United States get its full advantage on that pledge, seen, himself being witness, that that pledge has wrought its perfect work for the Government of the United States—I say that the man who, having assisted in that pledge, and seen it fully vindicated and redeemed so far as the interests of the United States were concerned, would now propose to break it, is a man—I will be mild—(laughter) —is a man who ought not to be trusted with any public position. I was going to use stronger language.

Do you mean to say, it may be asked, that that particular pledge made in 1864 should stretch out to the crack of doom over the people, and bind them hand and foot in all generations in the future? I don't say any such thing. I am not looking upon all the generations of the future. I have learned, in a public life of some length, if we take care of the honor of this generation we will do our share, and as to the limit of the pledge, this is it: It is binding upon the people of the United States until the uttermost farthing of debt, for which it was made the foundation and corner-stone, shall be paid. [Applause.]

And then, leaving the banks and leaving the greenbacks, they tell us that the Republican party has over-taxed the people. I observe lately, as I have had reason to get some stray numbers of the leading Democratic paper, it is raising the cry that the people ought to be relieved from the immensely burdensome taxation now weighing them down and taxing the life out of them—taxation levied by the National Government that was oppressing them so. That will bear examination. The taxation of the United States is, in round numbers, two hundred and forty million dollars per annum—a pretty large sum—and in round numbers one hundred and thirty millions of it are raised from the Tariff, and one hundred and ten millions from Internal Revenue. Now, I shall esteem my visit to New York a very lucky one for myself if I shall be enlightened upon this point: " What particular portion of the taxation of the United States is it that is bearing down with oppression and severity upon any citizen?" I would like to be told what particular part of it. if repealed, would let him go forth freer and lighter next day. Just one. What is the taxation to-day?

I will take the Tariff first. What is the taxation to-day levied by the Tariff, that if repealed to-mor-row would make a great relief generally? I am not going into the question of Protection. I am taking the existing status of the last revenue charges. Has there ever been a time in the memory of any man present when woolens, cottons, sheetings, shirting and articles of domestic consumption and every-day wear were as cheap to the people of the United States as they are in this year of grace 1879? [Applause.] Now, I have not said that some articles are not rather dearer. But they are articles of luxury which are made dearer. Silks are dearer, velvets are dearer, laces are dearer, camel's-hair shawls are dearer. [Laughter.] But if a, lady needs a camel's-hair shawl, and her father or husband is able to pay $1,000 for it, he is able to chip in a little for the duty. [Applause.] Besides, you see, a thousand-dollar camel's-hair shawl is not absolutely essential to a lady's respectability here, or her salvation hereafter. [Applause.] Now, on these articles of luxury, not of use, it is the Republican party who are responsible for the tariff. I don't want to dodge any of these things. For that existing status the Republican party is answerable; it was responsible, and takes the credit for it. Well, on this matter. they are willing to open the books.

Generally, I find a man very much oppressed with the tax on coffee. We took that off in June, 1872. [Laughter.] Prior to that time we had been getting $8,000,000 a year out of it; and under the demand for a free breakfast table men thought it wise and patriotic. Men, who think they know a great deal more than any body else, insisted that it was the unanimous demand of the American people that the tax be removed, so we took the tax off of coffee. And six months after that the wise and beneficent ruler of Brazil, finding that it didn't pay either an export or an import duty, finding that the tax had been taken off in this country, thought that it would pay to look after that article, and he decided to put on an export duty. [Laughter.] Then, after looking into the glass twice, we perceived that we had been legislating $8,000,000 out of the Treasury of the United States, and put that handsome sum into the Treasury of Brazil. [Laughter.]

And so it would be just the same with sugar. We had a large duty on sugar—very large, quite enormous—$38,000,000 or $40,000,000; the people of America have a very sweet tooth. [Laughter.] If the statistics of the Custom House are correct since General Arthur left it (great cheering and applause) —if they are right, the people of the United States used 1,800,000,000 pounds of sugar last year, which is about forty pounds for every man, woman, and child and baby in the country. If the people of the United States were to take off that tax, Spain which has exhausted its intellect and ingenuity for a century to wring the last dollar out of Cuba, would see whether it could not bear an export tax. And so in the end, in the case of sugar as in the case of coffee, if we took the duty off we would be letting the tax go into the Treasury of Spain instead of into our own, leaving the price the same to the American consumer. [Applause.]

So I want the papers to tell us what tax we are to take off, in order that the people of the United States may find relief. I want the *Tribune* or any other paper to instruct me, or the Democrats, as it has done (applause), for I am in search of knowledge on the Tariff. [Laughter.]

Again, take another instance. A man said to me once: "Why, look at the tax on railroad iron; isn't it at a tremendous figure?" I replied that I didn't then care to go into an exhaustive discussion on the question of Free-Trade or Protection. I could say, however, that as far as I was concerned, I was a Protectionist. [Applause.] Well, I said to this gentleman: "Certainly the tax looks a little heavy; but now, as an experienced man in that branch of the industries of the country, tell me your private opinion—tell me what the price of iron would have been only for this tax, if the tax had not fostered this enormous iron interest in the country, and thus created the great competition in the market from England at the present day. Why, we would have been at their mercy and allowed them, if they had control of the subject in their hands, to put up the price to whatever figure they chose. How do you think now, my friend, the price would have been to-day?" He then admitted that he supposed he would not have been able to get the iron as cheap as he did. [Applause.]

So much for the Tariff. Now as to another matter. Is anybody distressed with the internal revenue? [Laughter.] I have said that in round numbers $110,000,000 were the returns of the internal revenue. Last year we had $113,000,000 and I say that every dollar reached the Treasury. [Great cheering.] Considering the fact that it came through Collectors and Deputy-Collectors, and assistants and messengers in various forms and departments—a good many in all—and it happened to reach its proper destination at the right time, we ought to take heart and courage and believe that there is some honesty left in this wicked world yet. [Laughter.] It is a little healthier than the better, purer and honest days of the Republic when the Democrats ruled the Treasury. They used to allow $14 on every $1,000 for picking and stealing. [Great laughter.] Well, now, this $113,000,000, where does it come from? $103,500,000 of it, which is nearly all of it, comes from the whisky and tobacco trade.

Do you regard that as particularly oppressive in New York? [Laughter.] We rather enjoy it down in Maine, and I will tell you here just how to avoid paying any of it, because this tax is a peculiar one. This tax is not like the tax on your farm or house or stock, because you need not pay a solitary penny of it unless you choose, and if you do not drink, if you do not chew, or if you do not smoke, you go entirely free of the tax. It is not exactly a case of paying your money and having your choice, but you make your choice and then pay your money. [Laughter.]

Joking aside, this tax is a wise one. The elder Napoleon, who was statesman as well as warrior, said that he found that the two vices of the use of spirits and of tobacco paid him 300,000,000 francs, and he had never found two virtues in the Empire that paid it so well. [Applause.] And, my friends, I will say for myself that if you show me two such virtues I will vote for them myself. We get it, and get it easily, and we get it without the oppression of any human being.

I found in some sections of Ohio, down in the Hocking Valley coal regions, where General Ewing was speaking a little while ago (laughter), that they had the match tax. [Laughter.] There was great oppression from the match tax. Well, I found that down in Maine, wherever Greenbackism prevailed, they were impressed with the idea that the people were suffering an untold and cruel oppression from the match tax. I asked a man one day whom I met about this tax. I asked, " How many matches do you use in your family?" " Well," he said, " two gross?" and he answered so promptly that I knew that he came prepared. [Great Laughter.] I said, "did you ever count how many there are in two gross?" "well," he replied, " one gross is one hundred and forty-four and two gross is two-hundred and eighty-eight, and there being one-hundred matches in each box, that makes twenty-eight thousand eight hundred matches, and that's about eighty matches a day," I asked him: " Now don't you think that that number of matches takes an almighty amount of scratching?" [Great laughter.] I am used to country audiences, and if I overshoot or undershoot the mark in the presence of city folks, you will attribute it to my country education. [Renewed laughter.] But take the average farmer and I should suppose thirty boxes of matches would be a very abundant supply, and the family using thirty boxes is taxed to the extent of one-thirteenth of a cent a day, and I submit to you what I did to the people of Maine, that considering the trouble that Columbus had in finding this continent, and the trouble that Washington had in founding the Republic, and Grant and Sherman and Lincoln, or Lincoln, Grant and Sherman had in putting down the Rebellion, that the average American citizen will still hold on to the Federal Government, despite the one-thirteenth of a cent. [Laughter and applause.]

There never was any greater nonsense than to talk about the taxes of the United States being oppressive. I do not know anything about your State taxes —that is Governor Robinson's business. [Laughter and applause.] Those I do not touch. There is not a solitary financial issue on which the Republican party has taken ground since the beginning of the war, and especially since its conclusion, on which time and circumstance and truth have not vindicated them. [Great applause.] Not one. I for one would step out of the camp at any time, if any Democrat of respectability would tell me of one solitary issue, on which the Republicans have taken ground and put into the form of legislation, in which they have not been vindicated both by the facts and in the judgment of the American people. [Great applause.] A single instance. You know we were harried to death all over the country, platforms fulminated, orators reiterated, resolutions "resoluted" (laughter) on the subject of the taxation of bonds, and you were assured that the fate of the country hung upon it. The Republican party took the ground that they could not be taxed. They took the ground that it was not wise to tax them. [Applause.]

[At this point some one in the audience shouted from the rear of the hall, " Speak up, James, we can't hear." The remark occasioned an outburst of laughter lasting for some time, which Mr. Blaine appeared to enjoy heartily.] The Republican party, he continued when the uproar was ended, took the ground that the bonds of the United States, even if they could be taxed, ought not to be taxed, and that the result of it would be against the interests of every man, rich and poor, in the country. And now, instead of standing to claim at the end of this agitation that the Democrats have abandoned it—instead of standing here to claim that the bonds of the United States ought to be exempt longer from taxation, I stand here to say that the bonds of the United States pay a larger share of the taxation of this country than any other form of investment; and that under the policy of the Republican party that has come to pass, they are placed

as the one form of property which does pay the taxes
of the country.   A single moment on that.

Out where that gentleman interrupted me so pleas-
antly just now I see three conservative-looking men
—or rather, two not so conservative—that look like
three men down in Maine who are about to invest
$10,000 apiece.   One of them, the most conservative,
who is willing to take any interest if he can have it
safe, thinks he can take the United States bonds.
To be sure, $400 a year for $10,000 does not look
very large, but he is willing to take it, and he does take
it, and buys $10,000 of the bonds of the United
States and takes them home. and lets everybody
know it.   Right next him stands a gentleman who
says he can go down in Wall Street and get a thing
just as good as United States bonds, and realize 6
per cent.   He can buy, he says, State bonds, good
State bonds, and so, as he prefers 6 per cent. to 4, he
puts his $10,000 in· those bonds.   And there is
another gentleman a little beyond who takes his $10,-
000 and says there are a great many bonds, first-class
railways and so on, that pay 7 per cent.; so he puts
his money in them and gets 7 per cent.   Now, I take
it for granted that in a city like New York, with so
many churches, and as full of piety as a city must be,
so near to Brooklyn (laughter), that at the moment
those gentlemen who had invested their $10.000 in 6
and 7 per cent. bonds. get them, they will go right to
the assessor the next day and inform him of the fact.
I see by your silent acquiescence that this is a universal habit in New York. [Laughter.]   Down in
the country where we don't know so much, we don't
always find the way to the assessor's office. [Re-
newed laughter.]

Now, gentlemen, levity aside, suppose these investments actually made, and the three gentlemen go
home and lock up their three investments in their
safes, and they say nothing to any one. At the end
of the year which of these three men has paid his
taxes? That is the question I beg to submit. The
man who agreed to have it taken out at the beginning
and discounted at the office, or the man who takes
the whole of his interest, dodges the assessor, and
locks it up in his safe? Suppose to-day, as the Democrats have clamored for two or three years—making
it a part of their National platform—suppose that by
a meeting the bonds of the United States be declared
subject to taxation to-morrow; of course you would
have no longer four per cent., you would get six, an
increase of two per cent. on the amount of the issue,
which would be paid back by taxation. Suppose you
do make them taxable, would you expect that those
who invested in them would form in a long proces-
sion, singing as they go, " We're the chaps that have
got them." [Loud laughter.] There is no property
in the world that is so easy to evade taxation.
You know how they are kept. Generally in a little
tin trunk, securely deposited in the safe. And if a
man happen to be discovered in the possession of
them, nineteen chances out of twenty, the man says
they belong to his brother who is out in the diggings
of Colorado, or his son who is grazing out West, or
his brother's widow, now educating her children in
Europe. [Laughter.] They would be anybody's except those in whose possession they are found, and
the result would be that if this idea was put in force
the Government of the United States would be
mulcted $35,000,000 per annum.

11

I mentioned this not as a living question, because
it is past, but as a leading one on which the Democrats hounded us for twelve years, and to show that
the Republican party has been vindicated to the last
letter and figure in a policy which the people approve.
I repeat, if the Democrats will show a single feature
and single measure in the financial policy of the Republican party, in any form, which has not been approved by the people—if they will show a single
measure which has been passed, in the demagogue
language that is so frequently used, " in the interest
of the bondholder," as distinguished from the interest
of the people, and the obligations of National honor,
I will agree to withdraw my weak point altogether.
It is not much, but it is all I have to offer.

About February 20th last, the House of Representatives at Washington, under the control of the Democrats, sent to the Senate of the United States, which
was then Republican, two Appropriation bills.   One
was for the Army, and the other for the support of the
Legislative and Judicial and Executive Departments
of the Government, containing the salaries for the
payment of all the civil officers of the United States
in all the great departments of that Government.
These bills were not in the usual form.   They con-
tained certain conditions which the Democratic House
said to the Republican Senate must be complied with,
or else that Democratic House would not appropriate
any money for the support of the Government.   If I
had not spoken so long, I would give you five-min-
utes recess in order to take in the length and breadth
and heighth and depth of that abounding impudence.
[Laughter.]   Here was a Democratic House, entirely
in the control of the Southern wing of that party

that said to the Republican Senate: "There are certain statutes of the United States that we don't like. We are not able to repeal them unless you agree to it, and we don't know any way to make you agree to it, excepting by letting you know that we propose to choke the Government of the United States until you, willing to take it from its last gasp, will consent and submit to our demands." [Laughter.]

Well, the Republican Senate, although only Republican by two majority, was a pretty stiff body, and in as polite language as high temper would admit, they advised the House that they did not propose to take the bills on those conditions, and so the session of Congress closed without any appropriations being made for these great departments of the Government of the United States. And thereupon the President of the United States, as in plain duty bound, called Congress together in extra session; and then by the transmutation in political strength the Democrats had both houses of Congress. And then the game changed a little. Prior to the 4th of March it had been an attempt on the part of a Democratic House to bull-doze the Republican Senate. and now they thought that a Democratic House and a Democratic Senate might unite and bull-doze a Republican President. And so, after a proper debate, these measures were passed. They passed the Appropriation bills, and they put these riders or attachments or conditions upon these bills, and after they had been properly debated they were sent to the President. And when they reached the President he seems to have had open before him the Constitution of the United States, just at that section where it says that every bill having passed both houses of

Congress shall be sent to the President, and if he approve he shall sign it, but if he do not approve he
shall return it to the House in which it originated
with his objections.   The President applied it with
great literalness; in fact he returned it to the House
in which it originated with his objections.   [Laughter
and applause.]

And then they tried him again, and still the Constitution would fly open just at that point, and the
President returned it again.   [Laughter.]   And then
they tried it in a modified form, sliding down a little,
a third time, and still the President saw objections to
his signing it and returned it with those objections.
And then, in a little bit of a case, they tried it a
fourth time and failing, with both branches united, to
bull-doze the President, this great roaring Democratic
party which came in so full of courage and menace,
breathing out threatenings and slaughter on all who
should oppose it, went out like a little snarling, dis-
contented spaniel, with his tail between his legs, snarling and biting considerably and threatening to renew
the fight next year.

The people of the United States are a very practical people, and they have a natural curiosity to know,
and have been trying to find out just what these laws
were, that the Democrats proposed to suspend the
functions of the Government unless they could have
them repealed.   Well, I shall not repeat statutes to you.
I think I can tell you in brief what they were.   At the
same time I don't think I need to tell you what they
were; because if there be any spot in the United
States, that ought instinctively to know what they
were and are, it is this City of New York.   In the
country we understand it to be, what in the city you

call an open secret, that in 1868 the vote of the City
of New York which elected Seymour over Grant and
Hoffman over Griswold was a fraud, and it was given
by fraud. ["That's so!" and applause.] Congressional investigation exposed that fraud. A distinguished Senator of New York stated on the floor of
the Senate, that the investigation had exposed such
remarkably phenomenal voting that, in the old Sixth
Ward—the "Bloody Sixth" we used to call it by
way of pet name—that in the old "Bloody Sixth"
the whole Democratic majority in that year—the
Democratic majority—I don't mean the Democratic
vote—was larger in number than all the men, women,
children, babies, horses, cats and dogs together.
[Laughter.] Well, the Republican party thought
that this kind of voting ought to be stopped, and
that when it came to be practised at the elections of
Representatives to Congress it was high time for
Congress to do something. So they passed the iniquitous Election Law—iniquitous in the judgment of
the Democratic party—this cruel, tyrannical law that
I said I would explain to you. That terribly tyrannical law, if I understand it aright, says that in cities
of 20,000 or upwards, whenever a Representative to
Congress or Presidential Elector is to be chosen, if
there be ten men who think they cannot have a fair
election under the State laws, they may apply to the
Circuit or United States District Judge, and that
Judge under this terrible law shall appoint two supervisors for each polling place; and in order to
make the law tyrannical beyond endurance, these
supervisors shall be taken one from each party, and
then that they shall take their seats as State officers;
and these supervisors, carrying out the provisions of

the Republican enactment, shall see to it that every
man entitled to vote shall vote if he applies to do it,
and after his vote is in the ballot-box it shall be fairly
counted.   Think of that!

The Democrats one and all in 'Congress said they
couldn't live under that law. [Laughter.] They
said there were two objections: First, that the law
was in contravention of State Rights; and in the
next place, a more practical one was that if it stood
they would not carry the elections. [Laughter.] It
was on that that the fight took place. Now as to the
theory of this being a State-Rights question. Why,
if there be anything National it certainly is the election to the National Congress, and the express provision of the Constitution gives to Congress the right
to regulate that if it chooses.   And when you are attempting to hem that in, and confine it within the
narrow limits of State Rights, you are treading upon
the personal rights of every individual in the whole
country, because every member of Congress elected,
in far off and remote districts, has just as much and
just the same power over your interests as the ones
you choose in your own city.   The Representative of
the ward in which we are assembled has no more
power over the great and multiplied interests of the
vast emporium of trade than he who is elected in
Texas, or California, or Maine. Therefore every citizen
in every district of the United States has a right to
see and demand that every other district besides that
in which he himself votes shall have a fair and honest
election. [Loud and continued applause.]

That is the whole of this law. That is all there is
of it. It was not all there was of the discussion
(laughter,) because they attempted to mix up with it,

in a way to throw dust in the eyes of the people, the terrible charge that the Republicans were engaged in suppressing free suffrage and oppressing a free people by the use of the bayonet at the polls. And we had a six-weeks discussion over that, and during the whole of that discussion in the Senate, with a large Democratic majority, there was not one Senator who could say or would say that he had ever seen a United States soldier at the polls. [Applause.] Not one. Mr. Hereford, of West Virginia, a very candid gentleman, who would not misrepresent anything intentionally, thought he had some valuable testimony to give on the question, and it amounted to about this: That during an election a dozen years ago he "heerd tell" (great laughter) that a man who came from the adjoining county had "heerd tell," (renewed laughter) that over on the other side of the mountain range, where neither of them had been, there had been some troops used at the polls. But when we came to investigate the records at the War Department, we found that there never had been a soldier in West Virginia at all. [Laughter.] Senator Williams, of Kentucky, said he had seen troops at the polls in 1865. [Great laughter.] Very likely he did; they were pretty thick around at that time. [Laughter.] He saw them just as he was getting home from a four-years rebellion against the Government. [Applause.] I believe he could have said with a great deal more truth that he had seen more of them there a year before. [Laughter.] All the other Democratic Senators failed to respond. [Great laughter.] Mr. Bayard, a highly distinguished man of the Democratic party, could not say that there was a soldier in Delaware for fifteen years. [Laughter.]

Senator Thurman did not tell about the awful oppression resulting in Ohio from this cause, and so far as
the Democratic testimony went it was a singular kind
of evidence.

I had occasion to make a few remarks the other
evening in this place, after the speech of the distinguished Secretary of the Treasury; I called the attention of those present to the size and overwhelming
proportions of the Army of the United States.
[Laughter.] Its tremendous extent may be judged
when, filled up to the last regiment and last battalion
and company, it amounts to 25,000 men. [Applause.]
Its actual numerical strength is about 21,000. It is
the hardest-worked army on the face of the globe.
[Applause.] It has the vastest region to traverse
and to guard; it has the largest frontier line to
defend; it has the greatest number of infant settlements and adventurous frontiersmen away out
in the mountain ranges, passes, and defiles to
look after; it is an army, as I have said, that is
worked almost to death. They are all engaged out
there. And as I remarked here, if you draw a line
through Omaha north and south, and taking the
whole of that country that lies east of it, about 44,-
000,000 of people in thirty-two States, voting at 18,-
000 polling places, in 1,700 counties, there are just
1,132 troops to do the intimidating business. [Ap-
plause.] And that is all there is. And if we could
parcel those out in every State, North and South, east
of the Missouri River, all they could do would be to
march a ragged sergeant and corporal abreast throughout three counties. [Laughter.]

The numerical argument is a sufficient answer. It
is an utterly indefensible cry, for which there is no

justification in fact. There was never an army less disposed to interfere with the suffrage; there never was an army less disposed to interfere with what are political issues than the Army of the United States. [Great applause.] And yet, in the Senate of the United States, when the Democrats for six weeks were calling the attention of the country to this false and fraudulent cry, I ventured to test the sense of that body by offering an amendment which I thought at least had some value—I moved an amendment in these words —they were busy warning off the United States Army from where it had not chosen to interfere, and on that warning they desired to strip the President of the United States of the rightful command of the troops —" that at any election in any State for Representative in Congress or Presidential Elector, it shall not be lawful for any man to come to the polls armed with any weapon, either open or concealed (great applause), under penalty of a fine not less than five hundred dollars, nor more than five thousand dollars and imprisonment for not less than three months nor more than five years, or both at discretion." [Applause.] For I thought, and I think so the more and more I reflect on it, that if there be any day in the calendar in which there should be absolute immunity from all possibility of danger, it is that great day when the freemen of a free republic are summoned together to cast a free ballot. [Applause.]

And yet this Democratic Senate, that was so alarmed at the possibility of a couple of soldiers descending on three counties—this Democratic Senate, who had on their tables at that time the official proof, gathered by a committee of their own body, that in the election of the preceding year, 1878, thirty-eight

men had been murdered in connection with the elections of Louisiana and South Carolina alone—this
Democratic Senate, so solicitous, I say, to warn off
the Army that never fired a shot or raised a flag except in defence of the right (loud applause)—these
Democratic Senators, so anxious to warn off the legitimate authority of the Republic, could not find any
Constitutional power to say that the bloody-minded
Ku-Klux gang. that makes elections in the South
first a ghastly farce and then a still more ghastly
murder, should be stopped; and on the second offering of the amendment every solitary Senator on the
Democratic side voted against it.   And then the
Senator from Minnesota, Mr. Windom, took the
amendment, as I had brought it forward, and inserted
certain words so that it should read thus : "That it
shall not be lawful for any man to come to the poll,
armed with a deadly weapon. open or concealed, for
the purpose of interfering with another man's right
to vote " (" Hear, hear,"), making it the duty of the
prosecution—and as every lawyer would know, a
hard duty—to prove that the offender came with that
purpose.   And even with that defence for the wrong-
doer and extremely difficult task for the prosecution,
every Democratic Senator voted against it, voted
that the Ku-Klux should not be arrested, even with
that difficult proof to be obtained by the prosecution.

I would not dare to tell this story if there was not
a *Congressional Record*.   I think I know how to tell
the truth ; but I would not risk my individual ve-
racity on a question so extraordinary as that, if there
were not the stereotyped plates of the official report
of Congress, because it seems so absolutely incredi-
ble that in the nineteenth century, in the Senate of a

free Republic, that a majority of its members should be found to give that vote. [Applause.]

And these are the men that opposed, step by step, an Election Law which never assayed to do anything but secure equal rights to the voter; these are the men that said the Army of the United States, needed for the protection of citizens, of the settler and the frontiersman over a million square miles of infant tertitory, should never have one dollar for its support until the Republican President should sign that bill —which he didn't. These are the men that talked of the other great Department of the Government, and said there should not be a dollar appropriated for the Post-Office Department. A little inconvenient, to be sure, to the people of the United States, to close the Post-Office Department; but what is that compared with the importance of the Democratic party having an obnoxious Election Law wiped out? They said there should not be a dollar appropriated for the Pension Department. Two or three thousand families of maimed or dead soldiers are dependent. it is true, in whole or part, on the honorable beneficence of their Government; what is that compared to the demand of the Democratic party that a law which stands in the way of their carrying elections shall be wiped out? The pensioners can wait, and mayhap starve, in the interest of a Democratic victory. They said—and this is of interest to this great commercial metropolis—that there should not be a dollar appropriated for the Lighthouse Bureau, and that all this world of commerce, floating over 17,000 miles of coast and lake, and gulf and ocean, might go to destruction before they would appropriate a single dollar to light a single beacon.

I might go on enumerating the whole strength, power, benevolence, charity, good deeds of the Federal Government that were in these two bills, and this Democratic party said that these two bills should not be passed unless the Republican party, as a condition of their being passed, would agree by the signature of their President against his constitutional belief— would agree to the repeal of a law which as a party they did not like.]Applause.]

Now my friends, I think I am somewhat read in the political annals of this country. [Applause.] I defy any man in the history of this country from the early inception of the first steps of independence to this hour, in any popular assembly, State or National, to show me one solitary line of legislation that compares in infamy with that. [Great applause.] Senator Thurman, of Ohio, said that this was a happy country, a happy and prosperous country, until the Republicans got in, and then they disturbed everything. [Great laughter.] Well, the Republicans came into power in this country in 1861. That is the time they began to disturb things. [Laughter.] Eighteen years have since elapsed, and during this time the Republicans have disturbed things and destroyed the prosperity of the Republic. Why just please remember, that the property of the American people, added by themselves, to themselves, is larger in these eighteen years than all that had been created in the United States from the discovery of the continent by Columbus. Just remember, that in these eighteen years the articles exported from the United States are larger by $1,300,000,000 than all that was ever taken from our shores, from the Declaration of Independence down to the inauguration of Lincoln. Just remember, that the railways built in this country since Lincoln was inaugurated are as large, if not larger, than all the miles of railway in the civilized world at the day of his inauguration. [Applause.] That is the way we have been destroying the country. And during these eighteen years we have been afflicted with four years of war and six of financial depression. And now we are just entering upon another period of eighteen years. [Great applause.] And I want the young people of this assembly to get in Cooper Institute or some larger building at the end of those eighteen years in the year of grace 1897, and remember, if they remember my humble name at all, (cries of " Yes they will " and applause,) that I told them to-night that the wealth acquired in this country in those eighteen years would be larger than all that existed in the country to-day. [Applause.]

And now, my friends you have a duty to perform. You have an election next Tuesday. Senator Hendricks, in the late campaign in Ohio, in a formal speech, advised the people of the United States that whoever raised the cry of a Solid North was a traitor. [Laughter.] A fearful denunciation for Mr. Hendricks! [Laughter.] A Solid South is sweet to Mr. Hendricks' ears. I hope I shall live long enough to outlive the day of political division on the line between the South and the North. [Applause.] And I will tell you how, in my political faith, we shall outlive it. We shall outlive it by showing, in the might and majesty of a free people, that a Solid South shall not prevail in the acquirement of political power in this country. And we will put to flight and dispel the illusion of Democratic leaders about solidifying the Southern States and combining them

with a fragment of the North—in which fragment
they always include your imperial State—combining
them with a fragment of the North, and with this
combination governing the country. They mistake
the spirit of New York. [Applause.] For in that
contest New York will be as she was in the contest
in the field for the Union—she will be at the head of
that great column of States that stand for the Union
and for the rights of all. [Great applause.]

Now I want every man in New York, when he
votes on Tuesday next—or rather, before he votes—
to ask himself this simple question, "Whom do Jefferson Davis and Robert Toombs and their associates
desire to have elected Governor of New York?"
[Applause.] As between Kelly and Robinson they
haven't any choice. They would unite gleefully in
the chorus, "How happy I could be with either, were
'tother dear charmer away." [Laughter.] But not
one of them from the Potomac to the Rio Grande
wants Alonzo B. Cornell. And I want every man to
remember that in voting for Cornell he votes for the
best sentiments of the Republican party in its best
days. [Applause.] And I want them to understand
that in his support there are no divisions in the Republican party. There is no Hayes, no anti-Hayes in
the Republican party. [Applause.] It is a great
consolidated power, always at the front in the hour
of danger. It has led us in safety in dark and troub-
lous and perilous days, and on its success hangs the
fate of the American Union as that Union was designed to be by its founders. [Long and continued
cheering during which Mr. Blaine resumed his seat.]

The State election in Maine in September, 1878,
gave that State a Democratic and Greenback admin-.

istration, but the Republicans carried the election in September, 1879, electing Frank Davis, Governor. The Democratic State administration — Governor Garcelon and his Council—attempted to retain the control of the State in the hands of the Democrats and Greenbackers by counting out a number of Republican members of the newly elected Legislature on technical errors. During the last half of December, 1879, and the first half January, 1880, the State was almost on the verge of civil war and anarchy. But through the steadiness, persistence, and success with which Mr. Blaine conducted the Republican party through its troubles, he brought law and order out of chaos and threatened violence. No finer display of statesmanlike qualities has been seen in this country ,and the American people saw, in the protracted and perilous struggle in Maine, that Mr. Blaine exhibited all the qualities requisite for the discharge of the most difficult and delicate duties of an executive station.

The following is Senator Blaine's eulogy on the late United States Senator Zachariah Chandler, delivered in the United States Senate, January 28, 1880:

Mr. Chandler sprang from a strong race of men, reared in a State which has shed lustre on other Commonwealths by the gift of her native-born and her native-bred. She gave Webster to Massachusetts, Chief Justice Chase to Ohio, General Dix to New York, and Horace Greeley to the head of American journalism. Mr. Chandler left New Hampshire before he attained his majority, and with limited pecuniary resources sought a home in the inviting territory of the Northwest. He had great physical strength, with remarkable powers of endurance; possessed energy that could not be overtaxed; was gifted with courage of a high order; was imbued with principles which throughout his life were inflexible; was intelligent and well instructed; and in all respects equipped for a career in the great and splendid region where he lived, and grew, and strengthened, and prospered, and died.

For a long period following the second war with Great Britain the Territory of Michigan was governed by one of the most persuasive and successful of American statesmen, whose pure and honorable life, whose grace and kindness of manner, and whose almost unlimited power in what was then a remote frontier Territory, had enabled him to mould the vast majority of the early settlers to his own political views. When Mr. Chandler reached Detroit, General Cass had left the scene of his long reign—for reign it might well be called—to assume control of the War Department under one of the strongest administrations that ever governed the country. The great majority of young men at twenty years of age naturally drifted with a current that was so strong; but Mr. Chandler had inherited certain political principles which were strengthened by his own convictions as he grew to manhood, and he took his stand at once and firmly with the minority. He was from the outset a strong power in the political field; though not until his maturer years, with fortune attained and the harder struggles of life crowned with victory, would he consent to hold any public position. But he was in all the fierce conflicts which raged for twenty years in Michigan, and which ended in changing the political mastery of the State. It is no matter of wonder that personal estrangements occurred in such prolonged and bitter controversy, without indeed the loss of mutual respect, and in one of the most exciting periods of the struggle General Cass spoke publicly of not enjoying the honor of Chandler's acquaintance. It was just three years afterward, as Mr. Chandler delighted to tell with good-natured and pardonable boasting, that he carried to General Cass a letter of introduction from the Governor of Michigan, which so impressed the General that he caused it to be publicly read in this Chamber and placed on the permanent files of the Senate. It is to the honor of both these great men that complete cordiality of friendship was restored, and that in the hour of supreme peril to the nation which came soon after, General Cass and Mr. Chandler stood side by side in maintaining the Union of the States by the exercise of the war power of the Government. They sleep their last sleep, in the same beautiful cemetery, near the city which was so long their home, under the soil of the State which each did so much to honor, and on the shores of the lakes whose commercial development, spanned by their lives, has been so greatly promoted by their efforts.

The anti-slavery agitation which broke forth with such strength in 1854, following the repeal of the Missouri Compromise, met with partial reaction soon after, and in 1856 Mr. Buchanan was chosen to the Presidency. Mr. Chandler took his seat for the first time in this body on the day of Mr. Buchanan's inauguration. It was the first public station he had ever held except the Mayoralty of Detroit for a single term, and the first for which he had ever been a candidate, except when in 1852 he consented to lead

12

the forlorn hope of the Whigs in the contest for
Governor of Michigan. When he entered the Senate the Democratic party bore undisputed sway in
this Chamber, having more than two-thirds of the
entire body. The party was led by resolute, aggressive, able, uncompromising men, who played for a
high stake and who played the bold game of those
who were willing to cast all upon the hazard of the
die. The party in opposition, to which Mr. Chandler
belonged, was weak in numbers but strong in character, intellect, and influence. Seward, with his philosophy of optimism, his deep study into the working
of political forces, and his affluence of rhetoric, was
its accepted leader. He was upheld and sustained by
Sumner, with his wealth of learning and his burning
zeal for the right; by Fessenden, less philosophic
than Seward, less learned than Sumner, but more
logical and skilled o'fence than either; by Wade, who
in mettle and make-up was a Cromwellian, who, had
he lived in the days of the Commonwealth, would
have fearlessly followed the Protector in the expusiion
of an illegal Parliament. or drawn the sword of the
Lord and Gideon to smite hip and thigh the Amele-
kites who appeared anew in the persons of the cava-
liers; by Collamer, wise and learned, pure and dignified, conscript father in look and in fact; by John P.
Hale, who never faltered in his devotion to the anti-
slavery cause, and who had earlier than any of his
associates broken his alliance with the old parties,
and given his eloquent voice to the cause of the despised Nazarenes ; by Trumbull, acute, able, untiring,
the first Republican Senator from that great State
which has since added so much to the grandeur and
glory of our history ; by Hamlin, with long training,

with devoted fidelity, with undaunted courage, who came anew to the conflict of ideas with a State behind him, with its faith and its force, and who alone of all the illustrious Senate of 1857 is with us to-day; by Cameron, with wide and varied experience in affairs, with consummate tact in the government of parties, whose active political life began in the days of Monroe, and who, after a prolonged and stormy career, still survives by reason of strength at fourscore, with the strong attachment of his friends, the respect of his opponents, the hearty good wishes of all.

Into association with these men Mr. Chandler entered when in his forty-fourth year. His influence was felt, and felt powerfully from the first day. A writer at the time said, that the effect of Chandler's coming was like the addition of a fresh division of troops to an army engaged in a hand-to-hand conflict with an outnumbering foe. He encouraged, upheld, inspired, coerced others to do things which he could not do himself, but which others could not have done without him. His first four years in the Senate were passed in a hopeless minority, where a sense of common danger had banished rivalry, checked jealousy, toned down ambition, and produced that effective harmony and splendid discipline which won the most signal and far-reaching of all our political victories in the election of Abraham Lincoln to the Presidency. Changed by this triumph and the startling events which followed into a majority party in the Senate, the Republicans found many of their oldest and ablest leaders trained only to the duties of the minority, and not fitted to assume with grace and efficiency the task of administrative leadership. They had been so long studying the science of attack, that

they were awkward. when they felt the need and assumed the responsibility of defense. They were like
some of the British regiments in the campaign of
Namur, of whom William of Orange said there was
no fortress of the French that could resist them, and
none that was safe in their hands.

It was from this period that Mr. Chandler became
more widely known to the whole country—achieving
almost at a single bound what we term a national
reputation. His defiant attitude in the presence of
the impending and overwhelming danger of war; his
superb courage under all the doubts and reverses of
that terrible struggle between brethren of the same
blood; his readiness to do all things, to dare all
things, to endure all things for the sake of victory to
the Union; his ardent support of Mr. Lincoln's Administration in every war measure which was proposed; his quickness to take issue with the Administration when he thought a great campaign was about
to be ruined by what was termed the Fabian policy;
his inspiring presence, his burning zeal, his sleepless
vigilance, his broad sympathies, his prompt decision,
his eager patriotism: his crowning faith in the final
result, all combined to give to Mr. Chandler a front
rank among those honorable and devoted men who. in
our war history, are entitled to stand next to those
who led the mighty conflict on the field of battle.

To portray Mr. Chandler's career for the ten con-
secutive years after the war closed would involve too
close a reference to exciting questions, still in some
sense at issue. But in that long period of service,
and in the shorter one that immediately preceded his
death, those who knew him well could observe a constant intellectual growth. He was fuller and stronger

and abler in conference and in debate the last year of
his life than ever before.   He entered the Senate
originally without any practice in parliamentary discussion.   He left it one of the most forcible and
most fearless antagonists that could be encountered
in this Chamber.   His methods were learned here.
He was plain and yet eloquent; aggressive and yet
careful; fearless without showing bravado.   What he
knew, he knew with precision ; the powers he possessed were always at his command; and he never de-
clined a challenge to the lists. "Here and now" was
his motto, and his entire Senatorial career, and his
life outside indeed, seemed guided by that spirit of
bravery which the greatest of American Senators exhibited in the only boast he ever made, when he
quoted to Mr. Calhoun the classic defiance :

Concurritur ; horæ
Momento cita mors venit, aut victoria læta.

Mr. Chandler's fame was enlarged by his successful
administration of an important Cabinet position.
Called by President Grant to the head of the Interior
Department by telegraphic summons, he accepted
without reluctance and without distrust.   His eighteen
years of positive and uncompromising course in the
Senate had borne the inevitable fruit of many enmi-
ties, as well as the rich reward of countless friends.
The appointment was severely criticised and unspar-
ingly condemned by many who, a year later, were
sufficiently just and magnanimous to withdraw their
harsh words and bear generous testimony to his executive ability, his painstaking industry, and his inflexible integrity ; to his admirable talent for thorough organization, and to his prompt and graceful
dispatch of public business.   What his friends had

before known of his character and his capacity, the
chance of a few brief months in an administrative
position had revealed to his entire country, and had
placed in history.

It would not be just, even in the generous indulgence conceded to eulogy, to speak of Mr. Chandler
as a man without faults. But assuredly no enemy,
if there be one above his lifeless form, will ever say
that he had mean faults. They were all on the generous and larger side of his nature. In amassing his
princely fortune he never exacted the pound of flesh;
he never ground the faces of the poor; he was never
even harsh to an honest debtor unable to pay. His
wealth came to him through his own great ability,
devoted with unremitting industry for a third of a
century to honorable trade in that enlarging, ever-
expanding region, whose capacities and resources he
was among the earliest to foresee and to appreciate.

To his friends Mr. Chandler was devotedly true.
Like Colonel Benton, he did not use the word
"friend" lightly, and without meaning. Nor did he
ever pretend to be friendly to a man whom he did not
like. He never dissembled. To describe him in the
plain and vigorous Saxon which he spoke himself—
he was a true friend, a hard hitter, an honest hater.

In that inner circle of home life, sacred almost
from preference, Mr. Chandler was chivalric in devotion, inexhaustible in affection, and exceptionally
happy in all his relations. Whatever of sternness
there was in his character, whatever of roughness in
his demeanor, whatever of irritability in his temper,
were one and all laid aside when he sat at his own
hearthstone, or dispensed graceful and generous hos-
pitality to unnumbered guests. There he was seen

at his best, and there his friends best love to recall him. As Burke said of Lord Keppel, " He was a wild stock of pride on which the tenderest of hearts had grafted the milder virtues."

A sage, whose words have comforted many generations of men, tells us that when death comes, every one can see its deplorable and grievous side—only the wise can see causes for reconcilement. Let us be wise to-day, and celebrate the memory of a man who stood on the confines of age without once feeling its weakness or realizing its decay—who passed sixty-six years in this world without losing a single day of mental activity or physical strength ; who had a business career of great length and unbroken prosperity; who had attained in public life a fourth election to the Senate of the United States—an honor enjoyed by fewer men in the Republic than even its Chief Rulership; and who, strengthening with his years, stood higher in the regard of his countrymen, stronger with his constituency, nearer to his friends, dearer to his kindred, at the close of his career, than on any preceding day of his eventful life.

REPUBLICAN NATIONAL CONVENTION OF 1880.

The Presidential campaign of 1880 was now approaching. The most prominent candidates before the people for the Republican nomination were General U. S. Grant, James G. Blaine and John Sherman. General Grant had but recently returned from a three-years tour around the world and his political friends and admirers were ardent and persistent in pressing his claims before the country. The supporters of Senator Blaine were loudly enthusiastic in promoting the candidacy of their favorite. The adherents of

John Sherman, Secretary of the Treasury under President Hayes' Administration, were also earnest in furtherance of the pretensions of their candidate.

The movement for the nomination of General Grant for a Third Term was led by three United States Senators—Roscoe Conkling of New York, James Donald Cameron of Pennsylvania, and John A. Logan of Illinois. This Senatorial triumvirate formed the head of an alliance of the most formidable and aggressive character. Senator Cameron was absolute master in Pennsylvania, Senator Conkling had almost as firm a hold on New York, and Senator Logan was almost as thoroughly monarch of Illinois. These three men worked together for a common end, to serve their common ambition for political power, and victory seemed easily possible for them.

If they could not like Cæsar, Pompey, and Crassus, divide "this great empire" between them, they might jointly govern it through a man of their own selection, and each be secured in the absolute patronage of a State, so great as to be an empire in itself. General Grant was the fast friend of these three men, who were determined to nominate him for President, whether the people desired it or not. They had adroitly managed State conventions, packed with Grant delegates, and with these the three great leaders went to Chicago to force Grant's nomination.

Arrayed against the powerful Grant host were the friends of the other candidates for the Republican nomination. Three of these candidates were United States Senators: James G. Blaine, of Maine; George F. Edmunds, of Vermont, and William Windom, of Minnesota. John Sherman, President Hayes' Secretary of the Treasury, was also a candidate, as was also the Hon. Elihu B. Washburne, of Illinois.

Of all the candidates opposed to Grant the most powerful and the most popular was Senator Blaine. The Republican masses earnestly desired his nomination, and had no sympathy with the Grant Third-Term movement, however much they admired General Grant. Notwithstanding all the efforts of the Grant Senatorial triumvirate many of the States sent Blaine delegates to Chicago, and many of the leading newspapers in the country were enthusiastic in his support.

Wednesday, June 2, 1880, was the day, and Chicago was the place, fixed for the meeting of the Republican National Convention, to nominate candidates for President and Vice-President. That National Convention was one of the most important political conventions ever held in this country. It was the battle-ground on which several important questions—such as the unit rule, district representation, and the right of the people to elect their own delegates—were settled only after a hard-fought struggle.

Though one of the Grant leaders—Senator Cameron —was Chairman of the Republican National Committee, the majority of the Committee were opposed to Grant's nomination. By Monday, May 31, 1880— two days before the meeting of the National Convention—Chicago had filled up with delegates and politicians from all over the Union. To secure the unit rule—by which entire State delegations were bound to vote as instructed by their respective State Conventions, notwithstanding the preferences of individual delegates—the Grant leaders were fully com-

mitted, as it was necessary to do so in order to force
Grant's nomination. A meeting of the Republican
National Committee was accordingly hastily called at
the Palmer House. The anti-Grant men made an
effort to break down the unit rule, by which the delegates from New York, Pennsylvania and Illinois
were bound to obey Conkling, Cameron, and Logan.
The Committee's meeting was secret. As soon as the
Chairman, Senator Cameron, had called the Committee to order, William E. Chandler of New Hampshire,
one of the Blaine leaders, offered two resolutions recognizing the right of individual delegates to vote
according to their convictions, regardless of the
action of their respective State Conventions binding
them to vote as a unit.

The first resolution was adopted unanimously,
whereupon Chairman Cameron ruled the second resolution out of order, and refused to entertain an appeal from his decision. This high-handed action of
the Chairman struck the anti-Grant people with consternation. The Hon. Wm. P. Frye, of Maine, asked
the Chairman where he had learned parliamentary
law. Wm. E. Chandler announced that if the Chairman would not pay any respect to the Committee,
the same power that had made him Chairman would
remove him. The majority of the Committee being
opposed to Senator Cameron, appointed a committee
of six to nominate a Temporary Chairman, and the
Committee adjourned for a recess. During this recess
the determined purpose of the anti-Grant men to de-
pose Chairman Cameron was made apparent. The
crisis had been reached, and when the Committee
again assembled they had determined to deprive
Cameron of his power or exact from him a promise.

This plan was abandoned, Senator Cameron remaining obstinate in his position, and refusing to give any
promise that he would not enforce the unit rule, as
the Committee had it in their power to appoint an
acceptable Chairman. At midnight the Committee
adjourned; the Hon. George F. Hoar, of Massachusetts, was chosen Temporary Chairman, he being acceptable to the Grant men. For further protection,
a resolution was adopted before adjournment that
should Mr. Cameron be unable, through sickness or
any other cause, to present Mr. Hoar's name to the
Convention, Mr. Chandler, as chairman of the committee reporting his name, should do so. Amid the
intense excitement over these proceedings, the arbi-
trary action of Senator Cameron was warmly discussed by heated partisans. Eighteen of Cameron's
own delegation from Pennsylvania, and twenty-two
New York delegates signed protests against his arbi-
trary ruling.

Amid the wild excitement and bitter factional feeling over these proceedings, the Hon. Chester A.
Arthur, of New York, and the Hon. George C. Gor-
ham, of California, on behalf of the Grant men, submitted a proposition that Senator Hoar should be
accepted as Temporary Chairman of the Convention,
and that no attempt should be made to enforce the
unit rule, or have a test vote in the Convention,
until the Committee on Credentials had reported,
when the unit-rule question should be decided by the
Convention in its own way. After a long conference
of the anti-Grant men, this proposition was accepted
by all parties, and it was also agreed that the regular
delegates from Illinois and Louisiana should be admitted to participate in the Temporary Organization

of the Convention, and then take their chances with
the Committee on Credentials.

The Convention met in the morning of Wednesday, June 2, and during the afternoon session over
ten thousand people were within Exposition Hall. As
Senator Conkling strode down the aisle at the head
of the New York delegation, a simultaneous huzza
burst forth from the hall and galleries, and it speedily
broke out in a hearty applause. Senator Cameron
called the Convention to order with a short address,
and presented the name of Senator Hoar of Massachusetts as Temporary Chairman. Upon taking his
place as Chairman of the Convention, Senator Hoar
made a short speech. After the election of two
Secretaries, Eugene Hale, of Maine, moved for a call
of States, and the naming of the several members of
the Committees on Permanent Organization, Resolutions, Rules, and Credentials. When this was completed, Congressman Wm. P. Frye, of Maine, moved
that Utah be represented on the Credentials Committee, as it had been left off. Mr. Conkling objected,
but his point of order was over-ruled, and Utah secured her representation.

A far larger multitude filled Exposition Hall, when
the Convention met on Thursday morning, June 3,
and the anti-Grant people had secured a greater
representation in the spectators' seats and a better
location for their sympathizers. After the Convention had been called to order and prayer offered,
Senator Conkling moved for a recess, as the Credentials Committee were not ready to report. Eugene
Hale, backed by the cheers of the gallery, opposed
this motion. Mr. Conkling made a sarcastic sneer
at Mr. Hale and New England, to which Mr. Hale

quickly retorted, and was loudly applauded amid a gale of hurrahs. Mr. Conkling's motion was lost. A resolution offered by James F. Joy, of Michigan, a Blaine leader, allowing the contestants from Illinois to be heard before the Convention by such counsel as they desired, raised quite a storm, was declared lost by a *viva voce* vote, and after a demand for a roll-call, was withdrawn at Eugene Hale's request. A motion of General Sewell, of New Jersey, instructing the Committee on Permanent Organization to report, was adopted. The report continued Senator Hoar as Permanent Chairman, and provided for a Secretary and Vice-President from each State. After its reading and correction, Senator Hoar made a short address. A motion by Wm. P. Frye, of Maine, requesting the Committee on Rules to report brought Gen'l Sharpe, of New York, to his feet, who said he had no time to bring in his minority report. At Mr. Frye's request. General Garfield, the Chairman of the Committee on Rules, arose and was greeted with tremendous applause. Garfield's statement that Sharpe's motion was true, satisfied everybody, and Frye withdrew his motion. A sarcastic fling by Senator Conkling was answered by Mr. Frye. During the evening session a motion by Mr. Henderson, of Iowa, requesting a report from the Committee on Rules precipitated another clash between the opposing factions. and Senator Logan said that the Committee on Rules had agreed to wait until after the action on contested seats. After a discussion on this question by Messrs. Logan, Henderson, Boutwell of Massachusetts, Harrison of Indiana, Clarke of Iowa, Sharpe of New York, Garfield of Ohio, and Conkling, Mr. Sharpe's amendment instructing the Credentials Committee to re-

port was taken by yeas and nays. Senator Hoar's
announcement allowing an Alabama delegate to
vote 'no' contrary to the rest of the delegation
from that State was received with a tremendous
shout. This was a defeat of the obnoxious unit rule,
and other delegates voted their own convictions,
contrary to the instructions of their State conventions. Mr. Sharpe's amendment was rejected, which
was an overwhelming defeat for the Grant forces,
and the result was greeted with uproarious applause.
The three hundred and sixteen yeas represented the
strength of the Grant columns, and the four hundred
and six nays the strength of the anti-Grant men. On
motion of Mr. Brandagee, of Connecticut, Mr. Henderson's motion was then laid on the table. The
country was aroused to intense interest by these
proceedings. The Credentials Committee sat all night,
and decided in favor of the anti-Grant contestants
from Illinois, Louisiana, Pennsylvania, and other
States.

When the Convention assembled, on Friday morning, June 4th, Senator Conkling offered a resolution
binding the delegates to support the nominee of the
Convention whoever he might be, and expelling such
as refused to agree. After a few remarks by Eugene
Hale, Mr. Brandagee called for a vote of States. A
viva voce vote recorded half a dozen nays. On motion of Mr. Conkling a vote by States was taken, resulting in seven hundred and sixteen yeas and three
nays. Mr. Conkling then offered a resolution expelling the three delegates who had voted "no," and who
were from West Virginia. Mr. Campbell, of West
Virginia, defended his position in a short speech.
Mr. Hale, of the same State, who had voted "aye,"

defended Mr. Campbell's right to vote as he pleased. Mr. Brandagee denied this right. Mr. McCormick, of West Virginia, who had likewise voted "no," also defended his position. Mr. Garfield, amid great applause, spoke against Mr. Conkling's resolution of expulsion. After Mr. Pixley, of California, had moved to lay Mr. Conkling's resolution on the table, Mr. Conkling ordered a roll-call, but finally withdrew his resolution, amid applause and hisses. On motion of General Sewell, of New Jersey, the Committee on Rules reported. The rule forbidding any unit rule was loudly applauded. The minority report by Mr. Sharpe was buried in the adoption of the majority report. Mr. Conger, of Michigan, next presented the report of the Credentials Committee, which admitted the contesting delegates from Louisiana, Alabama, Illinois, Pennsylvania, and Kansas. The report was received with applause, and was another blow at the high-handed tactics of the Grant leaders. Mr. Clayton, of Arkansas, presented a minority report in favor of the sitting delegates. Mr. Conger moved to consider the Louisiana cases. Mr. Cessna, of Pennsylvania, moved to adopt that part of the report on which the whole committee agreed, and then consider the disputed issues, and was supported by Mr. Conkling. After a lively debate between Mr. Conger and Senator Logan, Mr. Cessna's amendment was unanimously adopted. Mr. Sharpe, of New York, had moved to strike from the report so much as related to the four Illinois delegates-at-large. Mr. Haymond, of California, opposed this, but Senator Logan supported Mr. Sharpe's motion, which was adopted.

During the evening session the question of contested seats was debated, and the mention of the

names of Grant and Blaine evoked prolonged applause. Mr. Boutwell, of Massachusetts, offered a
resolution substituting the minority report for the majority report, a resolution enforcing the unit-rule.
Mr. Conger rose to a point of order, and was sustained by the Chair. The Convention, by a *viva voce* vote,
decided overwhelmingly against Boutwell's resolution: and a division being demanded, resulted in a
vote of three hundred and six yeas to four hundred
and forty-nine nays. This settled the unit-rule
question, and was another decisive defeat for the
Grant forces. The majority report was then adopted.
A motion by Mr. Quarles, of Wisconsin, limiting
debate to one hour was opposed by Senator Logan.
Mr. Haymond, of California, followed in a speech, and
his allusion to Blaine provoked the most deafening
cheers and shouts. Mr. Conger and Elliot Anthony
spoke in favor of the Illinois contestants, and Mr.
Raum and Emery Storrs, of Illinois, for the sitting
delegates. Mr. Storrs' allusion to the names of Grant
and Blaine were vociferously cheered by their respective supporters. Senator Conkling, waving the banner
of the New York delegation, led the chorus of cheers
for Grant; and Robert G. Ingersoll, waving a lady's
shawl, was conspicuous in leading the cheering for
Blaine, which lasted many minutes. A lady in company with Marshall Jewell, of Connecticut, waved
two flags and repeatedly shouted "Hurrah for
Blaine!" For half an hour this uproar continued,
the enthusiasm of the Blaine people knowing no
bounds.

Exposition Hall was again packed on Saturday,
June 5, the fourth day of the Convention. When the
ten thousand people had got seated, Senator Conkling

strode down the centre aisle and was received with a thundering salute of applause.

After the Convention had been called to order, the Kansas case was settled in favor of the four Grant contestants, and the Illinois case in favor of the anti-Grant contestants, by a vote of four hundred and seventy-six to one hundred and eighty-four. The Sherman contestants from West Virginia were admitted by a vote of four hundred and seventeen to three hundred and twelve; and the Utah contestants by a vote of four hundred and twenty-six to three hundred and twelve. Mr. Garfield moved the adoption of the majority report, whereupon Mr. Sharpe moved to strike out the rule allowing delegates to vote contrary to the instructions of their respective State Conventions; and offered a resolution in favor of proceeding to ballot for a candidate for President. Mr. Garfield raised a point of order that the report of the Committee on Rules was before the Convention, and the Chair ruled Mr. Sharpe's motion out of order. A vote by a call of States was ordered, and Mr. Sharpe modified his resolution, which was still opposed by Mr. Garfield, and a dicussion on the rules followed between Messrs Frye, Garfield and Conkling.

Mr. Sharpe's resolution was lost by a *viva voce* vote, and afterwards by a call of States, which resulted in two hundred and seventy-six yeas to four hundred and seventy-nine nays. This result was hailed with great applause! Mr. Sharpe's motion to substitute the majority report was rejected. Amendments of the majority report concerning district representation in the next National Convention, offered by Mr. Boutwell, of Massachusetts, and Mr. Butterworth, of Ohio, were adopted by the Convention, which then adopted

13

the rules as a whole.   On motion of Mr. Garfield the
Committee on Resolutions then reported, and the Republican platform of 1880 was then read.   A civil-
service resolution offered by Mr. Barker, of Pennsylvania, precipitated a debate upon that question,
after which his resolution was adopted.

During the evening session, the spectators were
full of enthusiasm.   On motion of Eugene Hale, the
roll of States was called for the announcement of the
names of members of the Republican National Committee.   Mr. Hale next moved a call of States to
name candidates for President.   James F. Joy, of
Michigan, nominated Blaine in a speech, which was
vociferously applauded.   Mr. Pixley, of California,
seconded Blaine's nomination in a lengthy speech.
Senator Conkling nominated General Grant in a very
impressive speech, which was cheered for full twenty
minutes at its close.   Mr. Bradley, of Kentucky,
seconded Grant's nomination.

Mr. Garfield, of Ohio, nominated John Sherman,
in a very able speech, and this nomination was seconded by Mr. Winkler, of Wisconsin, and Mr. Eliott,
(colored,) of South Carolina.   Mr. Billings, of Ver-
men, nominated Senator Edmunds, and this nomination was seconded by Mr. Sanford, of Massachusetts.
Mr. Cassidy, of Wisconsin, nominated Elihu B.
Washburne, of Illinois, and this nomination was seconded by Mr. Brandagee, of Connecticut.   The Convention then adjourned over Sunday, having been in
session four continuous days.

On Sunday, June 6, 1880, at Chicago, the politicians were as busy as ever.   The day was passed in
marches and counter-marches, combinations, plots,
arguments, speeches, dining and wining, rest for some

and church for a few. Every nerve was strained to correct badly-constructed lines, to strengthen wavering delegates, and to capture new ones, and to repair every weak spot in the chain of defenses.

On Monday, June 7, Chicago was all astir, and vast crowds filled the halls, corridors, breakfast-rooms and street-corners. Exposition Hall was soon jammed with over ten thousand human beings. The various State delegations entered in the proper order. Senator Conkling was again vociferously applauded as he entered the hall and strode down the aisle. General Garfield was also royally welcomed when he entered. After Chairman Hoar had called the Convention to order, and after prayer, Eugene Hale, of Maine, moved that the Convention proceed to ballot for a candidate for President, and Senator Conkling seconded the motion. Eighteen ballots were taken during this session without any decisive result. During these eighteen ballots Grant's line stood firm. his vote ranging from three hundred and three to three hundred and nine; Blaine's friends also stood nobly by their favorite, with votes ranging between two hundred and eighty and two hundred and eighty-five; Sherman's adherents on the various ballots numbered from eighty-eight to ninety-five; Washburne's supporters mustered from thirty to thirty-six votes; Edmunds had between thirty-one and thirty-four votes on the different ballots; Windom had ten votes on each ballot. James A. Garfield, of Ohio, himself a delegate heading the Sherman delegation. had one and two votes between the second and thirteenth ballots inclusive. President Hayes had one vote on the tenth, eleventh and twelfth ballots. General Benjamin H. Harrison, of Indiana, grandson of

President Harrison, had one vote on the second ballot; Hon. Geo. W. McCrary, of Iowa, one vote on the thirteenth ballot; and Edmund J. Davis, of Texas, one vote on the seventeenth ballot.

During the ten ballots taken on Monday evening, June 7, Grant's vote ranged from three hundred and two to three hundred and seven; Blaine's from two hundred and seventy-five to two hundred and eighty-one; Sherman's from ninty-one to ninty-seven; Washburne's from thirty-two to thirty-six; Edmunds had thirty-one on each ballot, and Windom had ten on each ballot; while Garfield had one and two votes on the different ballots, and John F. Hartranft, of Pennsylvania, had one vote on the first four ballots of the evening session.

During the eight ballots of Tuesday, June 8th, Grant's columns stood as firmly by their candidate as ever, his vote ranging from three hundred and five to three hundred and thirteen. Blaine's adherents mustered from two hundred and seventy to two hundred and seventy-nine votes on the first six ballots of the day, but on the seventh ballot this vote fell to two hundred and fifty-seven, and on the last ballot to forty-two, most of his friends having stampeded to Garfield. Sherman's vote stood between ninety-nine and one hundred and twenty on every ballot but the last, when it fell as low as three. Washburne mustered from twenty-three to forty-four votes on every ballot but the last, when he only had five. Edmunds had twelve votes on the first ballot of the day, eleven on the next six, and none on the last. Windom had from three to seven on all the ballots of the day but the last, when he also had none. Garfield had one and two votes on the first five ballots of the day, seventeen and fifty respectively on the next two ballots, and three hundred and ninety-nine on the last ballot. Most of the supporters of Blaine, Sherman, Washburne, Edmunds and Windom had gone over to Garfield, thus giving him a majority of the Convention on the thirty-sixth and last ballot, and making him the nominee of the Republican party for President in 1880. The Grant Third-Term movement had utterly failed. The Blaine delegates, finding it impossible to nominate their candidate, had wheeled into line for Garfield as the only effective way of beating Grant. The result was greeted with tremendous applause; the vast crowd sang " The Battle Cry of Freedom," which the band was playing, while cannon were booming outside. Upon the announcement of Garfield's nomination, the vast crowd stood upon benches and hurrahed and yelled. Then Senator Conkling in a short speech moved that the nomination be made unanimous. Senator Logan then followed with a little address seconding the motion, as did also General James A. Beaver, of Pennsylvania. Eugene Hale then spoke on behalf of the Blaine men. Garfield's nomination was then made unanimous, amid the wildest excitement. During a short evening session on that day, Tuesday, June 8th, 1880, Chester A. Arthur, of New York, was nominated for Vice-President, after which the Convention adjourned *sine die*, after one of the most gigantic political struggles ever recorded. Mr. Blaine had not received the nomination, but he had been the means of defeating the Third-Term movement, so hostile to all the traditions of the Republic.

The following is a list of the thirty-six ballots, taken

during the two days—Monday, June 7th, 1880, and Tuesday, June 8th, 1880.

BALLOTS.	Grant.	Blaine.	Sherman.	Washburne.	Edmunds.	Windom.	Garfield.	Hayes.	Harrison.	McCrary.	Davis, Tex.	Hartranft.
Monday Afternoon, June 7.												
1st	304	284	93	30	34	10						
2d	305	282	94	31	32	10	1					
3d	305	282	93	31	32	10	1		1			
4th	305	281	95	31	32	10	1					
5th	305	281	95	31	32	10	1					
6th	305	280	95	31	32	10	2					
7th	305	281	94	31	32	10	2					
8th	306	284	91	32	31	10	1					
9th	308	282	90	32	31	10	2					
10th	305	282	92	33	31	10	1		1			
11th	305	281	93	32	31	10	2		1			
12th	304	283	92	33	31	10	1		1			
13th	305	285	89	33	31	10	1			1		
14th	305	285	89	35	31	10						
15th	309	281	88	36	31	10						
16th	306	283	88	36	31	10						
17th	303	284	90	36	31	10					1	
18th	305	283	91	35	31	10						
Monday Ev'g, June 7.												
19th	305	279	96	32	31	10	1					1
20th	308	276	93	35	31	10	1					1
21st	305	276	96	35	31	10	1					1
22d	305	275	97	35	31	10	1					1
23d	304	275	97	36	31	10	2					
24th	305	279	93	35	31	10	2					
25th	302	281	94	35	31	10	2					
26th	303	280	93	36	31	10	2					
27th	306	277	93	36	31	10	2					
28th	307	279	91	35	31	10	2					
Tuesday, June 8.												
29th ...	305	278	116	35	12	7	2					
30th	306	279	120	33	11	4	2					
31st ·····	308	276	118	37	11	3	1					
32d	309	270	117	44	11	3	1					
33d	309	276	110	44	11	4	1					
34th	312	275	107	30	11	4	17					
35th	313	257	99	23	11	3	50					
36th	306	42	3	5			399					

SECRETARY OF STATE.

The campaign of 1880 resulted in the triumphant election of Garfield, and upon his inauguration, March 4, 1881, Senator Blaine was appointed his Secretary of State. He at once distinguished himself by the vigor and earnestness with which he upheld American interests. He was the chosen adviser and confidential political and personal friend of President Garfield, whom he upheld in the bitter factional fight which soon disturbed the triumphant Republican party.

When President Garfield appointed William H. Robertson—the political rival of Senator Conkling in New York State—Collector of the port of New York, that Senator bitterly opposed the President's appointment in that instance, as he believed it was inspired by Senator Blaine. After considerable deliberation the United State Senate confirmed the appointments; and the two United States Senators from New York—Roscoe Conkling and Thomas C. Platt —resigned their seats in the Senate, and appealed to the Legislature of their State to sustain them in their opposition to President Garfield, by re-electing them to the seats which they had resigned; but after a bitter contest of two months, the New York Legislature sustained the President's course by defeating Messrs. Conkling and Platt, and electing Messrs. Miller and Lapham in their places.

In this struggle with Senator Conkling, President Garfield was sustained by the great mass of the Republican party throughout the country.

On the morning of July 2, 1881, President Garfield was shot in the Baltimore and Potomac Railroad Depot, in Washington, as he was about to take the

train, on his way to Williams College, where his son
was taking his educational course. Secretary Blaine
was walking with the President when the latter was
shot. The assassin Guiteau was speedily arrested and
taken to the Disirict jail, narrowly escaping lynching
by a mob.

Through all the period of eighty days of suffering
of the President, Secretary Blaine, the master-spirit
of the President's Cabinet, was virtually acting President; and after Garfield's death, and Vice-President
Arthur's inauguration as President, Mr. Blaine re-
mained in office for several months, but as he and the
new President differed on matters of public policy,
one point of which was Mr. Blaine's foreign policy,
the Secretary retired from office late in the Fall of
1881. Mr. Blaine's vigorous foreign policy—his demand for a modification, by Great Britain, of the
Clayton-Bulwer Treaty; his opposition to the course
of Chili in her victorious struggle with Peru; and
his project for a Congress of all the American Re-
publics to settle disputes—was not approved by President Arthur. Some time after his resignation Mr.
Blaine wrote a long letter to the President concerning
this foreign policy.

MR. BLAINE'S GREAT ORATION ON GARFIELD.

On February 27, 1882, Mr. Blaine delivered the following oration on the late PRESIDENT GARFIELD, before
both Houses of Congress and a vast multitude of
people, in the Hall of the House of Representatives,
in Washington:

MR. PRESIDENT: For the second time in this generation, the great Departments of the Government of the
United States are assembled in the Hall of Represen-

tatives, to do honor to the memory of a murdered President. LINCOLN fell at the close of a mighty struggle in which the passions of men had been deeply stirred. The tragical termination of his great life added but another to the lengthened succession of horrors which had marked so many lintels with the blood of the first-born. GARFIELD was slain in a day of peace, when brother had been reconciled to brother, and when anger and hate had been banished from the land. "Whoever shall hereafter draw the portrait of murder, if he will show it as it has been exhibited where such example was last to have been looked for, let him not give it the grim visage of Moloch, the brow knitted by revenge, the face black with settled hate. Let him draw, rather, a decorous, smooth-faced, bloodless demon; not so much an example of human nature in its depravity and in its paroxysms of crime, as an infernal being, a fiend in the ordinary display and development of his character."

From the landing of the Pilgrims at Plymouth till the uprising against Charles First, about twenty thousand emigrants came from Old England to New England. As they came in pursuit of intellectual freedom and ecclesiastical independence rather than for worldly honor and profit, the emigration naturally ceased when the contest for religious liberty began in earnest at home. The man who struck his most effective blow for freedom of conscience, by sailing for the colonies in 1620, would have been accounted a deserter to leave after 1640. The opportunity had then come on the soil of England for that great contest which established the authority of Parliament, gave religious freedom to the people, sent Charles to the block, and committed to the hands of Oliver Cromwell the su-

preme executive authority of England.   The English
emigration was never renewed, and from these twenty
thousand men, with a small emigration from Scotland
and from France, are descended the vast numbers
who have New England blood in their veins.

In 1685 the revocation of the Edict of Nantes by
Louis XIV scattered to other countries four hundred
thousand Protestants, who were among the most intelligent and enterprising of French subjects—merchants of capital, skilled manufacturers, and handi-
craftsmen, superior at the time to all others in Europe.
A considerable number of these Huguenot French
came to America ; a few landed in New England and
became honorably prominent in its history.   Their
names have in large part become Anglicised, or have
disappeared, but their blood is traceable in many of
the most reputable families, and their fame is perpet-
uated in honorable memorials and useful institutions.

From these two sources, the English-Puritan and
the French-Huguenot, came the late President—his
father, Abram Garfield, being descended from the one,
and his mother, Eliza Ballou, from the other.

It was good stock on both sides—none better, none
braver, none truer.   There was in it an inheritance of
courage, of manliness, of imperishable love of liberty,
of undying adherence to principle.   GARFIELD was
proud of his blood ; and, with as much satisfaction as
if he were a British nobleman reading his stately an-
cestral record in Burke's Peerage, he spoke of himself
as ninth in descent from those who would not endure
the oppression of the Stuarts, and seventh in descent
from the brave French Protestants who refused to
submit to tyranny even from the Grand Monarque.

GEN'L GARFIELD delighted to dwell on these traits,

and, during his only visit to England, he busied himself in discovering every trace of his forefathers in
parish registries and on ancient army rolls. Sitting
with a friend, in the gallery of the House of Commons one night, after a long day's labor in this field
of research, he said, with evident elation, that in every
war, in which, for three centuries, patriots of English
blood had struck sturdy blows for constitutional
government and human liberty, his family had been
represented. They were at Marston Moor, at Naseby,
and at Preston; they were at Bunker Hill, at Sara-
toga, and at Monmouth, and in his own person had
battled for the same great cause in the war which
preserved the Union of the States.

Losing his father before he was two years old, the
early life of GARFIELD was one of privation, but its
poverty has been made indelicately and unjustly
prominent. Thousands of readers have imagined him
as the ragged, starving child, whose reality too often
greets the eye in the squalid sections of our large
cities. GENERAL GARFIELD's infancy and youth had
none of their destitution, none of their pitiful features
appealing to the tender heart and to the open hand of
charity. He was a poor boy in the same sense in
which Henry Clay was a poor boy; in which Andrew
Jackson was a poor boy; in which Daniel Webster
was a poor boy; in the sense in which a large majority of the eminent men of America in all generations
have been poor boys. Before a great multitude of
men, in a public speech, Mr. Webster bore this testimony:

"It did not happen to me to be born in a log cabin,
but my elder brothers and sisters were born in a log
cabin raised amid the snow-drifts of New Hampshire,

at a period so early that, when the smoke rose first
from its rude chimney and curled over the frozen
hills, there was no similar evidence of a white man's
habitation between it and the settlements on the
rivers of Canada. Its remains still exist. I make to
it an annual visit. I carry my children to it to teach
them the hardships endured by the generations which
have gone before them. I love to dwell on the tender
recollections, the kindred ties, the early affections,
and the touching narratives and incidents which
mingle with all I know of this primitive family
abode."

With the requisite change of scene the same words
would aptly portray the early days of GARFIELD. The
poverty of the frontier, where all are engaged in a
common struggle, and where a common sympathy and
hearty co-operation lighten the burdens of each, is a
very different poverty, different in kind, different in
influence and effect from that conscious and humilia-
ting indigence which is every day forced to contrast
itself with neighboring wealth, on which it feels a
sense of grinding dependence. The poverty of the
frontier is indeed no poverty. It is but the beginning
of wealth, and has the boundless possibilities of the
future always opening before it. No man ever grew
up in the agricultural regions of the West where a
house-raising, or even a corn-husking, is matter of
common interest and helpfulness, with any other feeling than that of broad-minded, generous independence. This honorable independence marked the
youth of GARFIELD, as it marks the youth of millions
of the best blood and brain now training for the future citizenship and future government of the Republic. GARFIELD was born heir to land, to the title of

freeholder, which has been the patent and passport of self-respect with the Anglo-Saxon race ever since Hengist and Horsa landed on the shores of England. His adventure on the canal—an alternative between that and the deck of a Lake Erie schooner—was a farmer boy's device for earning money, just as the New England lad begins a possibly great career by sailing before the mast on a coasting vessel, or on a merchantman bound to the Farther India or to the China Seas.

No manly man feels anything of shame in looking back to early struggles with adverse circumstances, and no man feels a worthier pride than when he has conquered the obstacles to his progress. But no one of noble mould desires to be looked upon as having occupied a menial position, as having been repressed by a feeling of inferiority, or as having suffered the evils of poverty until relief was found at the hand of charity. General GARFIELD's youth presented no hardships which family love and family energy did not overcome, subjected him to no privations which he did not cheerfully accept, and left no memories save those which were recalled with delight, and transmitted with profit and with pride.

GARFIELD's early opportunities for securing an education were extremely limited, and yet were sufficient to develop in him an intense desire to learn. He could read at three years of age, and each winter he had the benefit of the district school. He read all the books to be found within the circle of his acquaintance; some of them he got by heart. While yet in childhood he was a constant student of the Bible, and became familiar with its literature. The dignity and earnestness of his speech in his maturer

life gave evidence of this early training. At eighteen
years of age he was able to teach school, and thence-
forward his ambition was to obtain a college education. To this end he bent all his efforts, working in
the harvest field, at the carpenter's bench, and, in the
winter season, teaching the common schools of the
neighborhood. While thus laboriously occupied he
found time to prosecute his studies, and was so successful that at twenty-two years of age he was able to
enter the junior class of Williams College, then under
the presidency of the venerable and honored Mark
Hopkins, who in the fullness of his powers, survives
the eminent pupil to whom he was of inestimable
service.

  The history of GARFIELD's life to this period presents
no novel features. He had undoubtedly shown per-
severience, self-reliance, self-sacrifice and ambition—
qualities which, be it said for the honor of our country, are everywhere to be found among the young men
of America. But from his graduation at Williams
onward, to the hour of his tragical death, GARFIELD's
career was eminent and exceptional. Slowly working
through his educational period, receiving his diploma
when twenty-four years of age, he seemed at one
bound to spring into conspicuous and brilliant success.
Within six years he was successively President of a
College. State Senator of Ohio, Major-General of the
Army of the United States, and Representative-elect
to the National Congress. A combination of honors
so varied. so elevated, within a period so brief and to
a man so young, is without precedent or parallel in
the history of the country.

  GARFIELD's army life was begun with no other military knowledge than such as he had hastily gained

from books in the few months preceding his march to the field. Stepping from civil life to the head of a regiment, the first order he received when ready to cross the Ohio was to assume command of a brigade, and to operate as an independent force in Eastern Kentucky. His immediate duty was to check the advance of Humphrey Marshall, who was marching down the Big Sandy, with the intention of occupying, in connection with other Confederate forces, the entire territory of Kentucky, and of precipitating the State into Secession. This was at the close of the year 1861. Seldom, if ever, has a young college professor been thrown into a more embarrassing and discouraging position. He knew just enough of military science, as he expressed it himself, to measure the extent of his ignorance, and with a handful of men he was marching, in rough winter weather, into a strange country, among a hostile population, to confront a largely superior force under the command of a distinguished graduate of West Point, who had seen active and important service in two preceding wars.

The result of the campaign is matter of history. The skill, the endurance, the extraordinary energy shown by GARFIELD; the courage he imparted to his men, raw and untried as himself; the measures he adopted to increase his force and to create in the enemy's mind exaggerated estimates of his numbers, bore perfect fruit in the routing of Marshall, the capture of his camp, the dispersion of his force, and the emancipation of an important territory from the control of the Rebellion. Coming at the close of a long series of disasters to the Union arms, GARFIELD's victory had an unusual and extraneous importance, and in the popular judgment elevated the young com-

mander to the rank of a military hero. With less
than two thousand men in his entire command, with a
mobolized force of only eleven hundred, without cannon, he had met an army of five thousand and defeated them—driving Marshall's forces successively
from two strongholds of their own selection, fortified
with abundant artillery. Major-General Buell, commanding the Department of the Ohio, an experienced
and able soldier of the regular army, published an
order of thanks and congratulation on the brilliant
result of the Big Sandy campaign, which would have
turned the head of a less cool and sensible man than
GARFIELD. Buell declared that his services had called
into action the highest qualities of a soldier, and
President Lincoln supplemented these words of praise
by the more substantial reward of a Brigadier-General's commission, to bear date from the day of his
decisive victory over Marshall.

The subsequent military career of GARFIELD fully
sustained its brilliant beginning. With his new commission he was assigned to the command of a brigade
in the Army of the Ohio, and took part in the second
and decisive day's fight in the great battle of Shiloh.
The remainder of the year 1862 was not especially
eventful to GARFIELD, as it was not to the armies with
which he was serving. His practical sense was called
into exercise in completing the task, assigned him by
General Buell, of reconstructing bridges and re-estab-
lishing lines of railway communication for the Army.
His occupation in this useful, but not brilliant, field
was varied by service on courts-martial of importance,
in which department of duty he won a valuable reputation, attracting the notice and securing the approval
of the able and eminent Judge-Advocate-General of

the Army. That of itself was warrant to honorable fame; for, among the great men who in those trying days gave themselves with entire devotion to the service of their country, one who brought to that service the ripest learning, the most fervid eloquence, the most varied attainments, who labored with modesty, and shunned applause, who in the day of triumph sat reserved, and silent, and grateful—as Francis Deak in the hour of Hungary's deliverance—was Joseph Holt of Kentucky, who in his honorable retirement enjoys the respect and veneration of all who love the Union of the States.

Early in 1863 GARFIELD was assigned to the highly important and responsible post of Chief-of-Staff to General Rosecrans, then at the head of the Army of the Cumberland. Perhaps in a great military campaign no subordinate officer requires sounder judgment and quicker knowledge of men than the Chief-of-Staff to the Commanding General. An indiscreet man in such a position can sow more discord, breed more jealousy and disseminate more strife than any other officer in the entire organization. When GEN'L GARFIELD assumed his new duties he found various troubles already well developed and seriously affecting the value and efficiency of the Army of the Cumberland. The energy, the impartiality, and the tact with which he sought to allay these dissensions, and to discharge the duties of his new and trying position, will always remain one of the most striking proofs of his great versatility. His military duties closed on the memorable field of Chickamauga, a field which, however disastrous to the Union arms, gave to him the occasion of winning imperishable laurels. The very rare distinction was accorded him of a great pro-

14

motion for his bravery on a field that was lost. President Lincoln appointed him a Major-General in the Army of the United States for gallant and meritorious conduct in the battle of Chickamauga.

The Army of the Cumberland was re-organized under the command of General Thomas, who promptly offered GARFIELD one of its divisions. He was extremely desirous to accept the position, but was embarrassed by the fact that he had, a year before, been elected to Congress, and the time when he must take his seat was drawing near. He preferred to remain in the military service, and had within his own breast the largest confidence of success in the wider field which his new rank opened to him. Balancing the arguments on the one side and the other, anxious to determine what was for the best, desirous above all things to do his patriotic duty, he was decisively influenced by the advice of President Lincoln and Secretary Stanton, both of whom assured him that he could, at that time, be of especial value in the House of Representatives. He resigned his commission of Major-General on the 5th day of December, 1863, and took his seat in the House of Representatives on the 7th. He had served two years and four months in the Army, and had just completed his thirty-second year.

The Thirty-eighth Congress is pre-eminently entitled in history to the designation of the War Congress. It was elected while the war was flagrant, and every member was chosen upon the issues involved in the continuance of the struggle. The Thirty-seventh Congress had indeed legislated to a large extent on war measures, but it was chosen before any one believed that the secession of the States would be actually attempted.   The magnitude of the work which fell upon its successor was unprecedented, both in respect to the vast sums of money raised for the support of the Army and Navy, and of the new and extraordinary powers of legislation which it was forced to exercise. Only twenty-four States were represented, and one hundred and eighty-two members were upon its roll. Among these were many distinguished party leaders on both sides, veterans in the public service, with established reputations for ability, and with that skill which comes only from parliamentary experience. Into this assemblage of men GARFIELD entered without special preparation, and it might almost be said unexpectedly. The question of taking command of a division of troops under General Thomas, or taking his seat in Congress, was kept open till the last moment—so late, indeed, that the resignation of his military commission and his appearance in the House were almost contemporaneous. He wore the uniform of a Major-General of the United States Army on Saturday, and on Monday, in civilian's dress, he answered to the roll-call as a Representative in Congress from the State of Ohio.

He was especially fortunate in the constituency which elected him. Descended almost entirely from New England stock, the men of the Ashtabula district were intensely radical on all questions relating to human rights.   Well educated, thrifty, thoroughly intelligent in affairs, acutely discerning of character, not quick to bestow confidence, and slow to withdraw it, they were at once the most helpful and most exacting of supporters.   Their tenacious trust in men in whom they have once confided, is illustrated by the unparalleled fact that Elisha Whittlesey, Joshua

R. Giddings, and JAMES A. GARFIELD represented the district for fifty-four years.

There is no test of a man's ability in any department of public life more severe than service in the House of Representatives; there is no place where so little deference is paid to reputation previously acquired, or to eminence won outside ; no place where so little consideration is shown for the feelings or the failures of beginners. What a man gains in the House, he gains by sheer force of his own character, and if he loses and falls back he must expect no mercy, and will receive no sympathy. It is a field in which the survival of the strongest is the recognized rule, and where no pretense can deceive and no glamour can mislead. The real man is discovered, his worth is impartially weighed, his rank is irreversibly decreed.

With possibly a single exception GARFIELD was the youngest member in the House when he entered, and was but seven years from his college graduation. But he had not been in his seat sixty days before his ability was recognized and his place conceded. He stepped to the front with the confidence of one who belonged there. The House was crowded with strong men of both parties ; nineteen of them have since been transferred to the Senate, and many of them have served with distinction in the gubernatorial chairs of their respective States, and on foreign missions of great consequence ; but among them all none grew so rapidly, none so firmly as GARFIELD. As is said by Trevelyan of his parliamentary hero, GARFIELD succeeded " because all the world in concert could not have kept him in the background ; and because, when once in the front, he played his part with a prompt intrepidity and a commanding ease that were but the outward symptoms of the immense reserves of energy, on which it was in his power to draw." Indeed the apparently reserved force which GARFIELD possessed was one of his great characteristics. He never did so well but that it seemed he could easily have done better. He never expended so much strength but that he seemed to be holding additional power at call. This is one of the happiest and rarest distinctions of an effective debater, and often counts for as much in persuading an assembly as the eloquent and elaborate argument.

The great measure of GARFIELD's fame was filled by his service in the House of Representatives. His military life, illustrated by honorable performance, and rich in promise was, as he himself felt, prematurely terminated, and necessarily incomplete. Speculation as to what he might have done in a field, where the great prizes are so few, cannot be profitable. It is sufficient to say that as a soldier he did his duty bravely; he did it intelligently; he won an enviable fame, and he retired from the service without blot or breath against him. As a lawyer, though admirably equipped for the profession, he can scarcely be said to have entered on its practice. The few efforts he made at the bar, were distinguished by the same high order of talent which he exhibited on every field where he was put to the test, and if a man may be accepted as a competent judge of his own capacities and adaptations, the law was the profession to which GARFIELD should have devoted himself. But fate ordained otherwise, and his reputation in history will rest largely upon his service in the House of Representatives. That service was exceptionally

long. He was nine times consecutively chosen to
the House, an honor enjoyed by not more than six
other Representatives of the more than five thousand
who have been elected from the organization of the
Government to this hour.

As a parliamentary orator, as a debater on an issue
squarely joined, where the position had been chosen
and the ground laid out, GARFIELD must be assigned
a very high rank. More, perhaps, than any man with
whom he was associated in public life, he gave careful and systematic study to public questions, and he
came to every discussion in which he took part with
elaborate and complete preparation. He was a steady
and indefatigable worker. Those who imagine that
talent or genius can supply the place, or achieve the
results of labor, will find no encouragement in GAR-
FIELD's life. In preliminary work he was apt, rapid,
and skillful. He possessed in a high degree the power
of readily absorbing ideas and facts, and like Dr.
Johnson, had the art of getting from a book all that
was of value in it by a reading, apparently so quick
and cursory, that it seemed like a mere glance at the
table of contents. He was a pre-eminently fair and
candid man in debate, took no petty advantage, stooped
to no unworthy methods, avoided personal allusions,
rarely appealed to prejudice, did not seek to inflame
passion. He had a quicker eye for the strong point
of his adversary than for his weak point, and on his
own side he so marshaled his weighty arguments as
to make his hearers forget any possible lack in the
complete strength of his position. He had a habit of
stating his opponent's side with such amplitude of
fairness and such liberality of concession that his followers often complained that he was giving his case

away. But never in his prolonged participation in the proceedings of the House did he give his case away, or fail in the judgment of competent and impartial listeners to gain the mastery.

These characteristics, which marked GARFIELD as a great debater, did not, however, make him a great parliamentary leader. A parliamentary leader, as that term is understood wherever free representative government exists, is necessarily and very strictly the organ of his party. An ardent American defined the instinctive warmth of patriotism when he offered the toast, "Our country, always right; but right or wrong, our country." The parliamentary leader who has a body of followers that will do and dare and die for the cause, is one who believes his party always right, but right or wrong, is for his party. No more important or exacting duty devolves upon him than the selection of the field and the time for contest. He must know not merely how to strike, but where to strike, and when to strike. He often skillfully avoids the strength of his opponent's position, and scatters confusion in his ranks by attacking an exposed point, when really the righteousness of the cause and the strength of logical intrenchment are against him. He conquers often both against the right and the heavy battalions, as when young Charles Fox, in the days of his Toryism, carried the House of Commons against justice, against its immemorial rights, against his own convictions, if, indeed, at that period Fox had convictions, and, in the interest of a corrupt administration, in obedience to a tyrannical sovereign, drove Wilkes from the seat to which the electors of Middlesex had chosen him and installed Luttrell in defiance, not merely of law but of public decency.

For an achievement of that kind Garfield was disqualified—disqualified by the texture of his mind, by
the honesty of his heart, by his conscience, and by
every instinct and aspiration of his nature.

The three most distinguished parliamentary leaders
hitherto developed in this country are Mr. Clay, Mr.
Douglas, and Mr. Thaddeus Stevens. Each was a
man of consummate ability, of great earnestness, of
intense personality, differing widely, each from the
others, and yet with a signal trait in common—the
power to command. In the give and take of daily
discussion, in the art of controlling and consolidating reluctant and refractory followers ; in the skill to
overcome all forms of opposition, and to meet with
competency and courage the varying phases of un-
looked-for assault or unsuspected defection, it would
be difficult to rank with these a fourth name in all our
Congressional history. But of these Mr. Clay was
the greatest. It would perhaps be impossible to find
in the parliamentary annals of the world a parallel to
Mr. Clay, in 1841, when at sixty-four years of age he
took the control of the Whig party from the President
who had received their suffrages, against the power
of Webster in the Cabinet, against the eloquence of
Choate in the Senate, against the Herculean efforts of
Caleb Cushing and Henry A. Wise in the House. In
unshared leadership, in the pride and plenitude of
power, he hurled against John Tyler with deepest
scorn the mass of that conquering column which had
swept over the land in 1840, and drove his Administration to seek shelter behind the lines of his political
foes. Mr. Douglas achieved a victory scarcely less
wonderful when, in 1854, against the secret desires of
a strong Administration, against the wise counsel of
the elder chiefs, against the conservative instincts and

even the moral sense of the country, he forced a reluctant Congress into a repeal of the Missouri Compromise. Mr. Thaddeus Stevens in his contests from
1865 to 1868 actually advanced his parliamentary
leadership until Congress tied the hands of the Pres-
dent and governed the country by its own will, leaving
only perfunctory duties to be discharged by the Executive. With two hundred millions of patronage in
his hands at the opening of the contest, aided by the
active force of Seward in the Cabinet, and the moral
power of Chase on the Bench, Andrew Johnson could
not command the support of one-third in either House
against the parliamentary uprising of which Thaddeus
Stevens was the animating spirit and the unquestioned
leader.

From these three great men GARFIELD differed
radically, differed in the quality of his mind, in temperament, in the form and phase of ambition. He
could not do what they did, but he could do what
they could not, and in the breadth of his Con res-
sional work he left that which will longer exert a
potential influence among men, and which measured
by the severe test of posthumous criticism, will secure a more enduring and more enviable fame.

Those unfamiliar with GARFIELD's industry and ignor-
rant of the details of his work, may, in some degree,
measure them by the annals of Congress. No one of the
generation of public men to which he belonged has contributed so much that will be valuable for future
reference. His speeches are numerous, many of them
brilliant, all of them well studied, carefully phrased,
and exhaustive of the subject under consideration.
Collected from the scattered pages of ninety royal
octavo volumes of *Congressional Record*, they would
present an invaluable compendium of the political

history of the most important era through which the National Government has ever passed. When the history of this period shall be impartially written, when war legislation, measures of reconstruction, protection of human rights, Amendments to the Constitution, maintenance of public credit, steps towards specie resumption, true theories of revenue may be reviewed, unsurrounded by prejudice and disconnected from partisanism, the speeches of GARFIELD will be estimated at their true value, and will be found to comprise a vast magazine of fact and argument, of clear analysis and sound conclusion. Indeed, if no other authority were accessible, his speeches in the House of Representatives from December, 1863, to June, 1880, would give a well-connected history and complete defense of the important legislation of the seventeen eventful years that constitute his parliamentary life. Far beyond that, his speeches would be found to forecast many great measures, yet to be completed—measures which he knew were beyond the public opinion of the hour, but which he confidently believed would secure popular approval within the period of his own lifetime, and by the aid of his own efforts.

Differing as GARFIELD does, from the brilliant parliamentary leaders, it is not easy to find his counterpart anywhere in the record of American public life. He perhaps more nearly resembles Mr. Seward in his supreme faith in the all-conquering power of a principle. He had the love of learning, and the patient industry of investigation, to which John Quincy Adams owes his prominence and his Presidency. He had some of those ponderous elements of mind which distinguished Mr. Webster, and which, indeed, in all our public life have left the great Massachusetts Senator without an intellectual peer.

In English Parliamentary history, as in our own, the leaders in the House of Commons present points of essential difference from GARFIELD. But some of his methods recall the best features in the strong, independent course of Sir Robert Peel, and striking resemblances are discernible in that most promising of modern conservatives, who died too early for his country and his fame, the Lord George Bentinck. He had all of Burke's love for the Sublime and the Beautiful, with, possibly, something of his superabundance; and in his faith and his magnanimity, in his power of statement, in his subtle analysis, in his faultless logic, in his love of literature, in his wealth and world of illustration, one is reminded of that great English statesman of to-day, who, confronted with obstacles that would daunt any but the dauntless, reviled by those whom he would relieve as bitterly as by those whose supposed rights he is forced to invade, still labors with serene courage for the amelioration of Ireland, and for the honor of the English name.

GARFIELD's nomination to the Presidency, while not predicted or anticipated, was not a surprise to the country. His prominence in Congress, his solid qualities, his wide reputation, strengthened by his then recent election as Senator from Ohio, kept him in the public eye as a man occupying the very highest rank among those entitled to be called statesmen. It was not mere chance that brought him this high honor. "We must," says Mr. Emerson, "reckon success a constitutional trait. If Eric is in robust health and has slept well, and is at the top of his condition, and thirty years old at his departure from Greenland, he will steer west and his ships will reach

Newfoundland. But take Eric out and put in a stronger and bolder man, and the ships will sail six hundred, one thousand, fifteen hundred miles farther and reach Labrador and New England. There is no chance in results."

As a candidate, GARFIELD steadily grew in popular favor. He was met with a storm of detraction at the very hour of his nomination, and it continued with increasing volume and momentum until the close of his victorious campaign :

> No might or greatness in mortality
> Can censure 'scape ; backwounding calumny
> The whitest virtue strikes. What king so strong
> Can tie the gall up in the slanderous tongue ?

Under it all he was calm, and strong, and confident ; never lost his self-possession, did no unwise act, spoke no hasty, or ill-considered word. Indeed nothing in his whole life is more remarkable or more creditable than his bearing through those five full months of vituperation—a prolonged agony of trial to a sensitive man, a constant and cruel draft upon the powers of moral endurance. The great mass of these unjust imputations passed unnoticed, and with the general *debris* of the campaign fell into oblivion. But, in a few instances, the iron entered his soul and he died with the injury unforgotten if not unforgiven.

One aspect of GARFIELD's candidacy was unprecedented. Never before, in the history of partisan contests in this country, had a successful Presidential candidate spoken freely on passing events and current issues. To attempt anything of the kind seemed novel, rash, and even desperate. The older class of voters recalled the unfortunate Alabama letter, in which Mr. Clay was supposed to have signed his political death-warrant. They remembered also the hot-tempered effusion by which General Scott lost a large share of his popularity before his nomination, and the unfortunate speeches which rapidly consumed the remainder. The younger voters had seen Mr. Greeley in a series of vigorous and original addresses preparing the pathway for his own defeat. Unmindful of these warnings, unheeding the advice of friends, GARFIELD spoke to large crowds as he journeyed to and from New York in August, to a great multitude in that city, to delegations and deputations of every kind that called at Mentor during the summer and autumn. With innumerable critics, watchful and eager to catch a phrase that might be turned into odium or ridicule, or a sentence that might be distorted to his own or his party's injury, GARFIELD did not trip or halt in any one of his seventy speeches. This seems all the more remarkable, when it is remembered that he did not write what he said, and yet spoke with such logical consecutiveness of thought, and such admirable precision of phrase, as to defy the accident of misreport and the malignity of misrepresentation.

In the beginning of his Presidential life GARFIELD's experience did not yield him pleasure or satisfaction. The duties that engross so large a portion of the President's time were distasteful to him, and were unfavorably contrasted with his legislative work. "I have been dealing all these years with ideas," he impatiently exclaimed one day, "and here I am dealing only with persons. I have been heretofore treating of the fundamental principles of government, and here I am considering all day whether A or B shall be appointed to this or that office." He was earnestly seeking some practical way of correcting the evils arising from the distribution of overgrown and unwieldy patronage—evils always appreciated and often discussed by him, but whose magnitude had been more deeply impressed upon his mind since his accession to the Presidency. Had he lived, a comprehensive improvement in the mode of appointment, and in the tenure of office, would have been proposed by him, and with the aid of Congress no doubt perfected.

But, while many of the Executive duties were not grateful to him, he was assiduous and conscientious in their discharge. From the very outset he exhibited administrative talent of a high order. He grasped the helm of office with the hand of a master. In this respect, indeed, he constantly surprised many who were most intimately associated with him in the Government, and especially those who feared that he might be lacking in the executive faculty. His disposition of business was orderly and rapid. His power of analysis and his skill in classification enabled him to dispatch a vast mass of detail with singular promptness and ease. His Cabinet meetings were admirably conducted. His clear presentation of official subjects, his well-considered suggestion of topics on which discussion was invited, his quick decision when all had been heard, combined to show a thoroughness of mental training as rare as his natural ability and his facile adaptation to a new and enlarged field of labor.

With perfect comprehension of all the inheritances of the war, with a cool calculation of the obstacles in his way, impelled always by a generous enthusiasm, GARFIELD conceived that much might be done by his Administration towards restoring harmony between the different sections of the Union. He was anxious to go South and speak to the people. As early as April he had ineffectually endeavored to arrange for a trip to Nashville, whither he had been cordially invited, and he was again disappointed a few weeks later to find that he could not go to South Carolina, to attend the Centennial Celebration of the victory of the Cowpens. But for the autumn he definitely counted on being present at three memorable assemblies in the South, the celebration of Yorktown, the opening of the Cotton Exposition at Atlanta, and the meeting of the Army of the Cumberland at Chattanooga. He was already turning over in his mind his address for each occasion, and the three taken together, he said to a friend, gave him the exact scope and verge which he needed. At Yorktown, he would have before him the associations of a hundred years that bound the South and the North in the sacred memory of a common danger and a common victory. At Atlanta, he would present the material interests and the industrial developments which appealed to the thrift and independence of every household, and which should unite the two sections by the instinct of self-interest and self-defense. At Chattanooga, he would revive memories of the war only to show that, after all its disaster and all its suffering, the country was stronger and greater, the Union rendered indissoluble, and the future, through the agony and blood of one generation, made brighter and better for all.

GARFIELD's ambition for the success of his Administration was high. With strong caution and conservatism in his nature, he was in no danger of attempting rash experiments or of resorting to the empiricism of statesmanship. But he believed that renewed and closer attention should be given to questions affecting the material interests and commercial prospects of fifty millions of people. He believed that our continental relations, extensive and undeveloped

as they are, involved responsibility, and could be cultivated into profitable friendship, or be abandoned to
harmful indifference or lasting enmity. He believed
with equal confidence, that an essential forerunner to
a new era of national progress must be a feeling of
contentment in every section of the Union, and a
generous belief that the benefits and burdens of government would be common to all. Himself a conspicuous illustration of what ability and ambition
may do under republican institutions, he loved his
country with a passion of patriotic devotion, and
every waking thought was given to her advancement.
He was an American in all his aspirations, and he
looked to the destiny and influence of the United
States with the philosophic composure of Jefferson,
and the demonstrative confidence of John Adams.

The political events which disturbed the President's
serenity for many weeks before that fateful day in
July form an important chapter in his career, and, in
his own judgment, involved questions of principle
and of right which are vitally essential to the Constitutional administration of the Federal Government.
It would be out of place here and now to speak the
language of controversy ; but the events referred to-
however they may continue to be a source of conten,
tion with others, have become, so far as GARFIELD is
concerned, as much a matter of history as his heroism
at Chickamauga or his illustrious service in the
House. Detail is not needful, and personal antago-
nism shall not be rekindled by any word uttered to-
day. The motives of those opposing him are not to
be here adversely interpreted nor their course harshly
characterized. But of the dead President this is
to be said, and said because his own speech is for-
forever silenced, and he can no more be heard except

through the fidelity and the love of surviving friends. From the beginning to the end of the controversy he so much deplored, the President was never for one moment, actuated by any motive of gain to himself or of loss to others. Least of all men did he harbor revenge, rarely did he even show resentment, and malice was not in his nature. He was congenially employed only in the exchange of good offices and the doing of kindly deeds.

There was not an hour, from the beginning of the trouble till the fatal shot entered his body, when the President would not gladly, for the sake of restoring harmony, have retraced any step he had taken if such retracing had merely involved consequences personal to himself. The pride of consistency, or any supposed sense of humiliation that might result from surrendering his position, had not a feather's weight with him. No man was ever less subject to such influences from within or from without. But after most anxious deliberation and the coolest survey of all the circumstances, he solemnly believed that the true prerogatives of the Executive were involved in the issue which had been raised, and that he would be unfaithful to his supreme obligation if he failed to maintain, in all their vigor, the Constitutional rights and dignities of his great office. He believed this in all the convictions of conscience when in sound and vigorous health, and he believed it in his suffering and prostration in the last conscious thought which his wearied mind bestowed on the transitory struggles of life.

More than this need not be said. Less than this could not be said. Justice to the dead, the highest obligation that devolves upon the living, demands the declaration that in all the bearings of the subject,

15

actual or possible, the President was content in his
mind, justified in his conscience, immovable in his
conclusions.

The religious element in Garfield's character was
deep and earnest. In his early youth he espoused
the faith of the Disciples, a sect of that great Baptist
Communion, which in different ecclesiastical estab
lishments is so numerous and so influential through.
out all parts of the United States. But the broadening
ing tendency of his mind and his active spirit of inquiry were early apparent, and carried him beyond
the dogmas of sect and the restraints of association.
In selecting a college in which to continue his education he rejected Bethany, though presided over by
Alexander Campbell, the greatest preacher of his
church. His reasons were characteristic: first, that
Bethany leaned too heavily toward slavery; and,
second, that being himself a Disciple and the son of
Disciple parents, he had little acquaintance with people of other beliefs, and he thought it would make him
more liberal, quoting his own words, both in his religious and general views, to go into a new circle and
be under new influences.

The liberal tendency which he anticipated as the
result of wider culture, was fully realized. He was
emancipated from mere sectarian belief, and with
eager interest pushed his investigations in the direction of modern progressive thought. He followed
with quickening step in the paths of exploration and
speculation so fearlessly trodden by Darwin, by Hux-
ley, by Tyndall, and by other living scientists of the
radical and advanced type. His own church, binding
its disciples by no formulated creed, but accepting
the Old and New Testaments as the word of God with
unbiased liberality of private interpretation, favored,

if it did not stimulate, the spirit of investigation. Its members profess with sincerity, and profess only, to be of one mind and one faith with those who immediately followed the Master, and who were first called Christians at Antioch.

But however high GARFIELD reasoned of "fixed fate, free will, foreknowledge absolute," he was never separated from the Church of the Disciples in his affections and in his associations. For him it held the Ark of the Covenant. To him it was the gate of Heaven. The world of religious belief is full of solecisms and contradictions. A philosophic observer declares that men by the thousand will die in defense of a creed, whose doctrines they do not comprehend and whose tenets they habitually violate. It is equally true that men by the thousand will cling to church organizations with instinctive and undying fidelity, when their belief in maturer years is radically different from that which inspired them as neophytes.

But after this range of speculation, and this latitude of doubt, GARFIELD came back always with freshness and delight to the simpler instincts of religious faith, which, earliest implanted, longest survive. Not many weeks before his assassination, walking on the banks of the Potomac with a friend, and conversing on those topics of personal religion concerning which noble natures have an unconquerable reserve, he said that he found the Lord's Prayer and the simple petitions learned in infancy infinitely restful to him, not merely in their stated repetition, but in their casual and frequent recall as he went about the daily duties of life. Certain texts of scripture had a very strong hold on his memory and his heart. He heard, while in Edinburgh some years ago, an eminent Scotch preacher who prefaced his sermon with reading the eighth chapter of the Epistle to the Romans, which book had been the subject of careful study with GARFIELD during all his religious life. He was greatly impressed by the elocution of the preacher, and declared that it had imparted a new and deeper meaning to the majestic utterances of St. Paul. He referred often in after years to that memorable service, and dwelt with exaltation of feeling upon the radiant promise and the assured hope with which the great apostle of the Gentiles was " persuaded that neither death, nor life, nor angels, nor principalities, nor powers, nor things present, nor things to come, nor height, nor depth, nor any other creature, shall be able to separate us from the love of God, which is in Christ Jesus our Lord."

The crowning characteristic of GENERAL GARFIELD's religious opinion, as, indeed, of all his opinions, was liberality. In all things he had charity. Tolerance was of his nature. He respected in others the qualities which he possessed himself—sincerity of conviction and frankness of expression. With him the inquiry was not so much what a man believes, but does he believe it? The lines of his friendship and his confidence encircled men of every creed, and men of no creed, and to the end of his life, on his ever-lengthening list of friends, were to be found the names of a pious Catholic priest and of an honest-minded and generous-hearted free-thinker.

On the morning of Saturday, July second, the President was a contented and happy man—not in an ordinary degree, but joyfully, almost boyishly happy. On his way to the railroad station to which he drove slowly, in conscious enjoyment of the beautiful morning, with an unwonted sense of leisure and a keen anticipation of pleasure, his talk was all in the grateful and gratulatory vein. He felt that after four months of trial his administration was strong in its grasp of affairs, strong in popular favor and destined to grow stronger ; that grave difficulties confronting him at his inauguration had been safely passed ; that trouble lay behind him and not before him ; that he was soon to meet the wife whom he loved, now recovering from an illness which had but lately disquieted and at times almost unnerved him ; that he was going to his Alma Mater to renew the most cherished associations of his young manhood, and to exchange greetings with those whose deepening interest had followed every step of his upward progress, from the day he entered upon his college course until he had attained the loftiest elevation in the gift of his countrymen.

Surely if happiness can ever come from the honors or triumphs of this world, on that quiet July morning, JAMES A. GARFIELD may well have been a happy man. No foreboding of evil haunted him; no slightest premonition of danger clouded his sky. His terrible fate was upon him in an instant. One moment he stood erect, strong, confident in the years stretching peacefully out before him. The next he lay wounded, bleeding, helpless, doomed to weary weeks of torture, to silence, and the grave.

Great in life, he was surpassingly great in death. For no cause, in the very frenzy of wantonness and wickedness, by the red hand of murder, he was thrust from the full tide of this world's interest, from its hopes, its aspirations, its victories, into the visible presence of death—and he did not quail. Not alone for the one short moment in which, stunned and dazed, he could give up life, hardly aware of its relinquishment, but through days of deadly languor, through weeks of agony, that was not less agony be-

cause silently borne, with clear sight and calm courage, he looked into his open grave. What blight and
and ruin met his anguished eyes, whose lips may tell
—what brilliant, broken plans, what baffled, high
ambitions, what sundering of strong, warm, manhood's friendships, what bitter rendering of sweet
household ties! Behind him a proud, expectant
nation, a great host of sustaining friends, a cherished
and happy mother, wearing the full, rich honors of
her early toil and tears; the wife of his youth, whose
whole life lay in his; the little boys not yet emerged
from childhood's day of frolic; the fair, young daughter; the sturdy sons just springing into closest com-
panionhip, claiming every day and every day the reward of a father's love and care; and in his heart
the eager, rejoicing power to meet all demands. Before him, desolation and great darkness! And his
soul was not shaken. His countrymen were thrilled
with instant, profound, and universal sympathy.
Masterful in his mortal weakness, he became the
centre of a nation's love, enshrined in the prayers of
a world. But all the love and all the sympathy
could not share with him his suffering. He trod the
wine-press alone. With unfaltering front he faced
death. With unfailing tenderness he took leave of
life. Above the demoniac hiss of the assassin's bullet
he heard the voice of God. With simple resignation
he bowed to the Divine decree.

As the end drew near, his early craving for the sea
returned. The stately mansion of power had been to
him the wearisome hospital of pain, and he begged to
be taken from its prison walls, from its oppressive,
stifling air, from its homelessness and its hopelessness.
Gently, silently, the love of a great people bore the
pale sufferer to the longed-for healing of the sea, to

live or to die, as God should will, within sight of its heaving billows, within sight of its manifold voices. With wan, fevered face tenderly lifted to the cooling breeze, he looked out wistfully upon, the ocean's changing wonders; on its far sails, whitening in the morning light; on its restless waves, rolling shoreward to brake and die beneath the noonday sun; on the red clouds of evening, arching low to the horizon; on the serene and shining pathway of the stars. Let us think that his dying eyes read a mystic meaning which only the rapt and parting soul may know. . Let us believe that in the silence of the receding world he heard the great waves breaking on a further shore, and felt already upon his wasted brow the breath of the eternal morning.

[The orator on concluding was greeted with most hearty applause, in which the whole audience joined.]

" Mr. Blaine is a man of good temper and temperament, though with a certain intellectual vehemence that might sometimes be mistaken for anger, of strong physique, wonderful powers of endurance and of recuperation, of great activity and industry, kindly and frank, easily approachable, and ready to aid all good causes with tongue, pen and purse. His studies have been largely on political questions and political history. Everything connected with the development of the country interests him, and he is a dangerous antagonist in any matter of American history—especially of the United States since the adoption of the National Constitution. He is an intense believer in the American Republic, one and indivisible, jealous and watchful for her honor, her dignity, and her right of eminent domain, ready to brave the wrath of the East for the welfare of the West, as in the Chi-

nese question ; ready to differ from political friends
rather than permit the indefinite suspension of the
writ of *habeas corpus ;* ready to brave the wrath of
the Conservatives for the rights of the Southern
blacks, as in his opposition to President Hayes'
Southern policy—and perfectly ready to give the
British lion's mane a tweak when that fine old king
of beasts crashes too clumsily among our fishing flakes.

" Mr. Blaine's knowledge of facts, dates, events,
men in history, is not only remarkable, but almost
unprecedented. In his college days he was noted for
his early love of American history, and for his inti-
mate knowledge of its details. That field of reading
has been enlarged and cultivated in all his subsequent
years, until it would be difficult to find a man in the
United States who can, on the instant, without reference to book or note, give so many facts and statistics relating to our financial and revenue system, to
our river and harbor improvements, to our public
lands, to our railway system, to our mines and min-
erals, to our agricultural interests—in fact, to everything that constitutes and includes the development,
achievement, and success of the United States. This
has been the study of his life, and his memory is an
encyclopœdia. He remembers because it is easier
than to forget."

Although Mr. Blaine had during the fall of 1882
declared his purpose not to be a candidate for the
Republican nomination in 1884, his partisans have
since been as ardent as ever in pushing his canvass
and keeping his name before the people. Since his
retirement from the Cabinet, Mr. Blaine has been engaged in literary pursuits, having written during this
period his *Twenty Years of Congress, from Lincoln
to Garfield, 1861 to 1881.*

www.ingramcontent.com/pod-product-compliance
Lightning Source LLC
Chambersburg PA
CBHW030126030726
47498CB00007B/2572